LORI WICK

THE CALIFORNIANS

HARVEST HOUSE PUBLISHERS

EUGENE, OREGON

Cover photos © Jose Luis Pelaez, Inc. / Blend Images / Getty; CampSpot / iStockphoto; Eva Serrabassa / iStockphoto

Cover by Terry Dugan Design, Minneapolis, Minnesota

SEAN DONOVAN
Copyright © 1993 by Lori Wick
Published by Harvest House Publishers
Eugene, Oregon 97402
www.harvesthousepublishers.com

ISBN-13: 978-0-7369-1947-0
ISBN-10: 0-7369-1947-3

Library of Congress Cataloging-in-Publication Data
  Wick, Lori.
    Sean Donovan / Lori Wick.
      p. cm.—(The Californians: bk.3)
Sequel to: Sean Donovan

ISBN: 1-56507-046-1

PS3573.I237S4   1993
813'.54—dc20

92-31560
CIP

Printed in the United States of America

07 08 09 10 11 12 13 14 15 / BC / 12 11 10 9 8 7 6 5 4 3 2 1

This book is dedicated to my nephews,
Derek Kolstad, Angus Wick, Bob Kolstad,
Billy Wick, and John Wm. Wick.
I pray that you will know God intimately,
and serve Him with your whole heart.

About the Author

Lori Wick was born and raised in Santa Rosa, California, the setting for this series. Lori and her husband, Bob, live in southern Wisconsin with their three children, Timothy, Matthew, and Abigail.

Visalia Families—1876

Sean Donovan

Charlotte Cooper (Charlie)
Sadie Cox (Charlie's Aunt)

Sheriff Lucas Duncan
    Wife—Lora

Santa Rosa Families—1876

The Marshall Riggs Family
    Wife—Kaitlin Donovan Riggs
    Children—Gretchen
               Molly
    Extended Family—Marcail Donovan

The William Taylor Family
    Wife—Mable (May)
    Children—Gilbert

The Jeffrey Taylor Family
    Wife—Roberta (Bobbie)
    Children—Cleo
               Sutton

The Nathan Taylor Family
    Wife—Brenda
    Children—William (Willy)

one

Santa Rosa, California
May 1874

That'll be it for the night, Sean. Close up the back and head home."

The brooding young man nodded but did not speak. It was on the tip of his tongue to tell the livery owner that he would go home if and when he felt like it, but that remark would probably cost him his job, and that was something he could not afford if he was ever going to get out of this town.

Carefully hiding his anger, Sean Donovan closed the rear doors of the livery with little more than a glance in the direction of his employer. He didn't speak or bid his boss goodnight, even as he made his way to the front door and out into the street. Dozens of other Santa Rosa residents were closing up shop and heading home. Many knew Sean by sight if not by name, but he chose to meet no one's gaze nor even return their greetings.

His sister's house loomed before him long before he was ready to face his family. He hesitated in the street for several minutes, hoping he could get upstairs to his bedroom without being noticed.

"Sean?" His sister called as soon as the front door opened, and Sean worked to conceal the anger he felt.

"Hi, Sean." A very pregnant Kaitlin Riggs came from the direction of the kitchen, her voice as sweet and kind as her spirit, but it was totally lost on Sean. "How was work?"

"Fine," he replied sullenly, and Katie found herself fighting to keep her own feelings from showing. All they did lately was quarrel, and Kate did not feel up to an argument tonight. She couldn't help asking herself, however, how long was he going to stay angry? How long were she and the family going to be made to suffer for something their father had done?

"Supper is nearly ready. Why don't you wash up?"

Sean turned to the stairs without answering her, walking straight past his younger sister, Marcail, without even acknowledging her.

Marcail and Kaitlin exchanged a look, but knew that more words wouldn't change anything. When they entered the kitchen together a moment later, Kate's husband was coming in the back door. Marshall Riggs, "Rigg" to everyone, pulled his wife close and kissed her. He then went to his sister-in-law to embrace her and kiss the top of her dark head.

"Where's Gretchen?" Rigg asked after his daughter, who was not quite two years old.

"She's playing on our bed," Katie answered him.

Rigg went in the direction of the bedroom, tossing the question over his shoulder as he went, "Did Sean get home?"

Kate answered softly, "He's here, Rigg. I can tell he doesn't want to be, but he's here."

❑ ❑ ❑

Sean lay on his bed waiting for his sister's call to supper. He didn't care to join the family any earlier than necessary. In fact, if Kate would let him, he'd eat alone in his room. No one in this house understood him. He hated school and he hated work. Their answer for everything was "trust in God." Well, he'd tried trusting in God, at least trusting Him to give the things he wanted most, but it never brought him anything more than pain and confusion.

With these restless thoughts, Sean stayed on the bed for only a few moments. Rolling to the edge of the mattress and standing in one move, he went straight to the dresser, opened the top drawer, and removed a wooden box. He counted the money within, knowing the exact amount but somehow hoping it had increased from when he had counted it the night before.

"Still not enough," Sean whispered, rage boiling within him as he replaced the box. "Still not enough to get away from here." Again his voice was whisper soft, but this time it held a hint of desperation.

He stood for some time trying to calm down, knowing that if Kate called now he would be too angry to join the family for supper and they would want to know why. Suddenly the door opened. Sean turned with a furious word for the intruder, but what he was going to say died in his throat at the sight of his niece Gretchen. She stood on the threshold, an adorable smile lighting her face.

For the first time that day, some of Sean's fury drained away. He held his arms out toward the beloved little girl and smiled as she threw herself at him. With her small arms circling his neck, she chatted up into his face. Sean, very much enamored with this child, gave her his full attention. They were still talking when Rigg's voice sounded from the bottom of the stairs.

"Gretchen, did you tell Uncle Sean that supper is ready?"

Gretchen, with a little hand to her surprised mouth, delivered the forgotten message, and the two of them made their way downstairs. Sean's face, all smiles for Gretchen, was now shuttered as the family gathered around the table. He did not close his eyes or even bow his head for the prayer.

Everyone save Sean talked with familiar ease throughout the meal. In the past Sean's silence had been oppressive and even intimidated the family, but now they had learned to live around it. Rigg, never intimidated by anyone, talked to his young brother-in-law as though nothing was out of the ordinary, including telling him to help with the dishes at the end of the meal. Rigg ignored the black scowl Sean sent in his direction.

"Do you want to wash or dry?" Rigg asked casually when the girls had emptied out of the room.

"I don't want to do either. Why can't Marc do—"

"That's enough, Sean," Rigg said easily. "She takes your turn more often than she should. And," Rigg spoke quickly when Sean opened his mouth yet again, "if you dare suggest that Kate come back in here, I'll flatten you. She could have the baby any time now and I don't—"

"Any time?" Sean's voice was incredulous. "I thought she was due in June."

"Sean," Rigg's voice was long-suffering. "There are only three days left in May. The doctor told Katie yesterday that it could be any time." Rigg wanted to add that if Sean would get his head out of his angry cloud and think about someone else for a change, he might have noticed how large and uncomfortable his sister had become.

Rigg would have been surprised to know that such words were unnecessary. Sean was giving himself the same speech. Unfortunately, he didn't believe his attitude to be his own fault; his father was to blame. If his father had kept just one of his promises, Sean believed he'd feel differently, but it was easier to blame his father than himself, and easier still to hide his pain behind a mask of fury.

□ □ □

The next evening, just after supper, Kate announced that they had received a letter from Father. Patrick Donovan, father to Kaitlin, Sean, and Marcail, was a missionary in the Hawaiian Islands. He'd been away and promising to come and see them for several years. Katie and Marcail had both suffered with his absence, but not to the same degree as Sean. When their mother had died just before Patrick left, Marcail and Kaitlin had clung to each other. But Sean, try as he might to fit in, had felt completely on his own.

"He says," Katie began, "that it looks like he'll be getting away in a few months. I'll read that part. 'I know I've said this before, but I'm sure I'll be able to break away from here and be with you by midsummer.'"

Kate fell silent then, praying that this time it would be true. So often he'd tried to come, but something always interfered. They were all beginning to believe that they would never see this man again; Sean was *hoping* he would never see his father again. Rigg, closely watching Sean's face, realized with a start that Sean actually wanted to avoid his father. That night in bed, the house quiet, Rigg said as much to Katie.

"I can't believe that, Rigg," Kate spoke in protest. "Sean has missed Father more than any of us. Seeing him again has been all he's living for."

"I understand what you're saying, Kate, but think about how betrayed he feels. You can feel his anger the moment he steps into the room. I don't want to upset you, but I thought you should be warned."

In the dim lantern light, Kate studied Rigg's face. "What are you *not* telling me," she finally asked.

"You might disagree with me, Kate, but I think he's trying to gain the courage to leave here. I think if he had the money, he'd walk away from Santa Rosa right now."

Kate's eyes grew to the size of saucers. "He has a box of money in the top drawer of his dresser," she whispered, as though afraid of being overheard. "I came across it by mistake just yesterday when I was putting his clothes away. The lid flipped up, and I saw what was inside. I closed the drawer right away, so I don't know how much there was, but—"

"Shhh," Rigg hushed her as she began to cry, his arms moving to surround her swollen frame. "It's all right, Kate. You didn't intrude. As hard as it seems, it just might need to be this way."

"Rigg, he's not ready to be out on his own," she sobbed.

"I realize that, but as you've said many times, he might need to go through more pain before he sees that God has been in control from the very start."

Kate was out of words then, as she cried and prayed into her husband's chest. Rigg held her until he fell asleep, only to be awakened once again, several hours later, with Kate telling him that he should probably go for the doctor.

two

The next afternoon Sean sat in his sister's room and held his niece Molly. She was a tiny dark-haired bundle, ten hours old and looking just like Gretchen had at that age. His sister was resting in the bed, and Sean was unaware of her scrutiny.

Help him turn to you, Heavenly Father, Kate prayed silently. *Help him see that running will do no good. If it be Your will, use this precious baby to soften him, to show him that you are a God of love and tenderness, especially when we hurt.*

Rigg entered the room then, and Sean's attention was drawn away from the sleeping infant. He surprised both parents with a compliment, something he hadn't given in ages.

"I don't know how you do it, Katie, being married to a great hairy beast like Rigg, but Molly is a beauty."

"Beauty runs in my family," Rigg told him, his voice amused.

Sean snorted in disgust and startled the babe in his arms. Kate watched in fascination as he spoke to Molly in soothing tones and held her even closer to his chest. Husband and wife exchanged a glance after witnessing this tender act, their hearts praying for the same thing.

❏ ❏ ❏

The next two weeks were nearly idyllic in Kate's esti-
mation. Molly was a good baby, and Sean was as civil as
she'd seen him in months. He was also very helpful and
unashamedly in love with his new niece. He played with
Gretchen every spare minute and appeared to be making
an effort to once again join the family. All of this changed
abruptly, however, when a letter came from Aunt Maureen in San Francisco.

She was bubbling over with excitement over Patrick's
promised arrival, really believing that this time he
would come. Kate read the letter to everyone after supper, and both she and Rigg took note of how tense Sean
became, how shuttered his features.

They talked that night and decided not to confront
Sean, but to keep their eyes open for a while and pray for
an opportunity to speak with him.

But no such opportunity arose. Rigg was at work,
Marcail was at school, and Kate was with the girls at
Grandma Taylor's house the day Sean wrote a brief note,
left it in his room, and walked to the other side of town to
catch a stage headed south. What never occurred to Sean
was that his actions were exactly like those of the man he
told his heart he most hated.

❑ ❑ ❑

Maureen Lawton Kent, sister to Patrick Donovan,
stood in her library trying to calm the frantic beating of
her heart. Her nephew Sean was upstairs in one of the
bedrooms, and she knew he would be coming back
down for supper at any moment. She wondered how
swiftly she could get word to Kaitlin and the family,
somehow certain that none of them knew where Sean
was. The thought had barely formulated when the subject of Maureen's thoughts appeared in the door.

Sean's appearance surprised her. He'd filled out even more from when she had seen him at Christmas, losing almost all of his boyish looks in the process. His brows were low over his unsmiling eyes, and his mouth, even when he spoke, was set in a grim line.

"Oh there you are." Maureen hated how breathless she sounded. "Are you ready for supper?"

Sean nodded and followed his aunt to the table. For the most part, the meal was silent and tense. Sean was starting to regret his decision to come here; in fact, he was starting to regret his decision to leave Santa Rosa. He knew he would have to force his family's faces from his mind or there would be more tears. Sean's anger rushed in and rescued him. There had been tears on the stage and then again in the room upstairs, but no more, he told himself.

Maureen, who was watching some of the emotions cross her nephew's face, quite frankly did not know what to say. He'd become a stranger since they were last together. By the time coffee was served she had gained some courage, telling herself that if he felt free enough to come here and live, then she was within her rights to ask a few questions.

"Sean," she began tentatively, "does your family know you're here?"

"No." He answered without looking at her.

"Won't they be worried?"

Sean shrugged. "I left a note saying I was leaving town. They'll have to be satisfied with that." It caused Sean more pain to say that than he let on, but Maureen was so surprised at his anger that she did not notice. In the face of that ire, some of her courage deserted her. A moment passed before she summoned a falsely cheerful voice and went on.

"Are you going to be looking for work?" Maureen's grown son, Percy, had lived off her income for years, so she did not take for granted that Sean would look for work.

"Not here. I don't like the weather." Sean said the first thing that came to mind, not wanting to admit that San Francisco was too close to Santa Rosa.

Maureen nearly panicked over his words. It never once occurred to her that he was just stopping off on his way through; in fact, she had a faint hope that he had come here because this was where his father's ship would be docking.

"Aren't you worried about missing your father's visit?"

Her question was met with a cold stare, and Maureen, so surprised at how far off her guesses had been, subsided into silence. Not many minutes passed before Sean took himself off to bed. In the hours before she went to bed herself, Maureen had a one-sided conversation with her absent brother. She told him in no uncertain terms that he should have come home ages ago, that letters had not been enough, and that his family needed him.

Maureen was utterly drained by the time she retired. Knowing how hard it would be to get to sleep, she tried to put her worries aside by telling herself that Sean might be more congenial in the morning. This was her last thought as sleep crowded in to claim her, but her hope was not to be realized. In the morning, Sean Donovan was gone.

three

Sean had lied about not liking San Francisco's cool temperatures in order to get away, but as he bent over another row of cotton in the hot Fresno sun, he found himself wishing he'd stayed a little longer. Never had he lived and worked in such high temperatures. Most of the other workers around him were shorter and for the first time, Sean envied them their small size. He had been picking crops for two weeks, and his back was still screaming at him.

He paused to wipe the sweat from his face and saw the very pregnant woman working next to him bending over the row with difficulty. She lost her balance, and Sean reached for her, taking her arm until she was once again steady on her feet. The smile she gave him was tired and sweet, and Sean hurriedly bent his head.

The sight of her and that fatigued smile caused him to think of Kaitlin just months before he left, and then of Molly just an infant when his stage left town. Sean suddenly felt like his emotions would choke him.

You've left, Sean, he said to himself, *and by now, they don't want you back. Even if they did, you don't want to go.* Convinced of this, he pushed the sight of Gretchen and

Molly from his mind. They were the last things he needed to be dwelling on right now.

"I wonder if *Father* made it home," Sean muttered to himself, bringing his anger to a head as he again bent his back.

Routine began to develop, and by the time Sean had been on the job for two months, he had made a few friends. Most of his co-workers were family men, but a few were single, and these were the men who took their pay to the bar as soon as it was placed in their hands.

Sean had never been in a bar, but he found the one in Fresno to be a place where he fit in. He never drank enough to become drunk, but the way he was left alone to sit in peace with his friends was just what he needed, or so he told himself. It was on one of these occasions that his co-workers told him he was in the wrong business.

"What are you talking about?" Sean frowned at them. He had been something of a mystery to them, but one night they'd coaxed his age out of him and realized he was just a kid with a chip on his shoulder. They grinned in his direction as they answered.

"Do you think we would be out picking crops if we were your size? Look at that guy at the end of the bar. You're bigger than he is, yet you're out there sweating in the sun with us."

"And probably getting paid a whole lot less for your effort," another man contributed, and the group roared with laughter. Sean didn't laugh; he was already moving down the long counter toward the end of the bar.

"What'll it be?" The bartender spoke without preamble.

"A job," Sean flicked his head in the direction of the strong-arm. "Any chance you're thinking of a change?"

The bartender was quick on the upswing, his eyes taking in the breadth of Sean's chest. He only smiled and shook his head no.

"I like Bear. He's not very bright, but he's reliable." Sean frowned and the man went on. "I'll tell you what I'll do, though. My brother owns a place in Selma, bigger than this, with a stage and girls and all. How old are you?"

"Old enough," was Sean's answer, and the smaller man behind the counter didn't press him.

"I'm sure you'll do. Head south a bit, downtown Selma. The place is called Buck's. Ask for either Buck, that's my brother, or his partner, Sal. They'll do right by you."

Sean's co-workers were ecstatic when he relayed the conversation, and for once Sean's face was not void of expression. He stayed long in the bar that night, laughing and talking with his friends in a kind of farewell celebration. Leaving just a few hours before dawn to return to the shabbiest hotel in town, he packed his few things and lay on the bed waiting for the sun to rise. When it did, Sean was up, shaved, and waiting for the stage that would yet again take him south.

❑ ❑ ❑

Four months later Sean, now eighteen years old and dressed in immaculate dark slacks, a snow white shirt, and dark tie, kept his eyes on his boss's profile. The men at the corner table were quickly growing out of hand, and Sean knew that any moment he would be called in. A woman came by, heavily made up, and seductively ran her hand across Sean's chest. As usual, he barely took notice of her.

Buck's head turned a moment later, and Sean went into action. He was only one of three bouncers in this posh establishment, and their movements were never to be hurried or ungainly. With natural grace Sean and one other man moved toward the rear. And with far less noise or action than one would have dreamed possible, the two troublemakers were extracted from the game and *shown* into the alley.

The show started moments later. Sean stood at one corner of the stage, his eyes constantly scanning the room for trouble. Tonight's crowd was raucous, but no one was out of control. At closing Sean made his way upstairs to his room with only the faintest feeling of dissatisfaction. He realized as he climbed into bed that he'd been spoiling for more of a fight. The men they'd taken into the alley had gone much too willingly.

He lay in the beautiful room he called his own and listened to the hotel bar grow quiet. Someone knocked on his door, but Sean didn't answer. It would only be one of the girls, asking if he'd changed his mind about joining her in her room. The answer was always no, and Sean had started ignoring the questions altogether.

They believed he thought himself too good for them, but that wasn't the case. In truth, Sean wasn't sure what held him back. He never hesitated to gamble or drink in the worldly environment in which he lived. His hesitance might have had to do with the fact that every time he was tempted, he saw his mother's face. She died when he was 14, but he could still hear her voice telling him when he was just 12 that saving himself for marriage must be a priority. "You'll never regret it, Sean, but if you don't wait, I can make you no such promise."

As usual, Sean didn't care for the direction of his own thoughts. Determined to sleep, he rolled to his side, shifting his thoughts to the stage downstairs with its heavy gold curtain and velvet trim. The name "Buck's" had given Sean an image of a rough-and-tumble bar, but

Buck's was more than a bar; it was a hotel, and a classy one at that.

Sean fell asleep telling himself that for the past three years he had been working too hard. This was the life he was meant to lead. This was where he belonged.

□ □ □

"I'm telling you, I don't like him," Sal told his partner.

"He's a good worker," Buck reasoned.

"He's too sure of himself," Sal went on. "I don't trust him."

Buck only sighed. He liked Sean Donovan, but Sal had never been comfortable with their new bouncer. Sal had wanted to fire him on several occasions when there was really no reason, but Buck had always forestalled him. Sean was the first strong-arm they hadn't had to teach to use a fork. Sean had class. Where he came from, and how he came to be working in a bar, Buck didn't care. All he knew was that Sean worked hard and made the place look good with his broad build, black curly hair, and dark compelling eyes. He didn't smile much, but he was always polite to the patrons, and Buck's clientele was his main concern.

"He stays," Buck said with finality. Sal, knowing he was needed on the floor, let the matter drop. He hoped though, that something would happen to give him a reason to sack Sean Donovan, one that not even Buck could dispute.

Two months later, Sean was once again in the mood for trouble. These feelings did not come on very often, but when thoughts of his past plagued him, he felt mean. On this particular day, he had thought of nothing but Marcail. She would be 13 by now and, with her dark hair and large expressive eyes, probably leading the boys on a merry chase.

"Rigg better be taking care of her," Sean said into the mirror as he tied his tie. He suddenly shook his head. All of this because one of the new show girls had smiled at him, a smile so sweet and young that Sean had been stunned. Marcail's face had immediately swum into view, invading his thoughts to a ridiculous degree so that by the time he went on duty, his temper was at its worst.

Early in the evening, a fight broke out. It seemed completely routine to all involved, but in his present mood, Sean was a bit too rough. Before anyone could guess what was about to happen, the man Sean had by the arm, threw a punch, and missed. Sean, trained to ignore such things, flattened the man. Within seconds several tables full of men were in a fight, and before a minute had passed, half the place was in an uproar.

Sal was thrilled with everything but the damage. Buck could see it was a losing battle this time: Sean would have to go. What neither Buck nor Sal understood at first was that it would have happened anyway. The first man Sean hit had been the sheriff's brother. Within the space of 12 hours, Sean was on yet another stage headed out of town.

four

Sean had not liked the look of the livery owner from the day they met, but he'd given him work and at the time that was all he wanted. The repairs at Buck's had nearly cleaned him out, and Sean knew that his money was not going to last long.

Sean came to Tulare thinking to find more work in a bar, but the owner of the place he tried had not been interested. It went against Sean's grain to be doing manual labor once again, but the future need for food and lodging had been at the back of his mind, and he had relented. That had been over two weeks ago, and Sean had yet to see a dime of his earnings.

In truth Sean enjoyed livery work, but he was still angry over the way he'd been treated at Buck's, and wouldn't have admitted this to anyone. Right now he was down to his last few coins and decided that today he would collect his pay. He dropped what he was doing, a sudden premonition coming on him, and went right then to seek out his boss.

"Get back to work." The obese, bald man spoke from a chair by the door.

"When do I get paid?"

"You haven't worked here long enough."

"I've been here two weeks," Sean's voice dropped to a dangerous note, but the fat man took no notice.

The big man laughed. "Come back when it's been a month."

"I'll take my pay now."

The man only laughed harder, now looking at Sean's flushed face. "You're a fool," the man chortled. "It wouldn't matter when you came, I don't have the money. The wife takes every dime." The man found this highly amusing and laughed as though he hadn't a care in the world.

Sean was furious. He started toward the man, intending to beat the money out of him, but a gun appeared in the livery owner's hand. Sean kept coming. It took a moment for the fat man to see that this time his scheme was not going to work. He scrambled to his feet, fear making him clumsy. Sean had the man backed into a stall when a voice interrupted him.

"Is there some problem?"

The voice stopped Sean's movement, but he didn't turn to see the man standing just inside the door.

"We're closed," Sean barked over one shoulder.

"Put the gun down, Pinky." The voice spoke again, not at all intimidated by Sean's anger. "Have you been cheating someone again, Pinky?"

This time the voice captured Sean's attention. He turned to find a small man dressed in a well-cut suit regarding him with an almost gentle smile. At the same time, the fat man, now behind Sean, began to babble.

"It's not my fault, Hartley. You know what she's like. I should send this guy over there and let him beat it out of her." The man sounded on the verge of tears, and Sean's face showed his disgust.

Without a word to either man, he strode to the back, picked up his jacket, and went out the door. In his anger it took some minutes for him to realize that someone was calling his name. He stopped and turned. Once again the small man, Hartley had been his name, was smiling at him and approaching with bold confidence.

"I'm sorry about what happened in there. Pinky is a disreputable worm, but compared to his wife he's an angel."

Sean had stayed silent through this recital, and Hartley spoke as though he'd suddenly remembered his manners.

"Where is my head," he said when he saw no answering smile in the younger man's eyes. "I'm Hartley. Pinky told me your name is Sean."

Sean stared for a moment at the offered hand but finally gave his own. "Sean Donovan."

He turned in the direction of his lodgings, and Hartley, with practiced ease, fell in step beside him.

"I'm not sure what your plans are for the rest of the day, Sean, but if you haven't a previous engagement, I'd like to take you to supper."

"Why?" Sean answered, stopping again and scrutinizing Hartley with eyes hard as flint.

"I have a business proposition for you."

Sean weighed this carefully, trying to gauge the man's honesty. His first thought was that the man was not the least bit honest, but there was something fascinating about him, and in a moment Sean found himself agreeing.

In an hour he had cleaned up and was walking through the door of the best hotel in town. Sean and Hartley were shown to a table as though they were royalty, and after Hartley ordered for them, he turned to Sean, again sporting that gentle smile.

"I will admit to you straight away, Sean, that I sought you out because of your size. You see, I'm in need of a personal bodyguard, and I think you might be the man."

Sean was quiet, and Hartley was relieved that he didn't ask what became of his last one. Hartley knew it would do nothing for his position if he had to admit that his last "bodyguard" died while they'd been robbing a bank. He was quite certain that Sean would eventually join him in his robberies, but now was not the time to go into that.

"What do you do for a living?"

"I'm in finance," Hartley told him smoothly. "There are times when I'm required to carry large sums of cash. I'm certain that having a man of presence with me will deter even the most persistent pursuers. Tell me, Sean, can you fire a gun?"

"No." Sean hated to answer because he suddenly wanted this job. This man, the way he was dressed, and the way he carried himself reminded him of Buck's, and Sean missed the class and excitement of that place.

"Well, no matter," Hartley assured him. "I can teach you."

Long before the meal ended, Sean's head was swimming with all that Hartley promised. For the last several weeks it seemed his luck had been bad, but now as he crossed the street with Hartley to a fancy bar, not as a worker but as a patron, Sean believed his luck had finally turned around.

❑ ❑ ❑

A sudden noise outside the door had Sean on his feet. Listening intently, he reached silently for his gun and made his way out to the living room. Not having bothered to dress, he eased the door open to the hall, but found the passageway outside their suite of rooms empty. He closed the door again, and went back to bed, telling himself he was taking his job too seriously.

It had been six weeks now since he had met Hartley, and never had he lived in such luxury. A niggling irritation that he wasn't doing much to earn his keep popped up in the back of his mind, but Sean effectively pushed it away. He now knew what Hartley was, and had to force himself to push that thought away as well.

He had always hated stealing, and even though he'd been well on the way to getting drunk, Hartley's news about being a professional thief had come very close to sobering him. That had been just two weeks ago, and Sean could see now how very carefully he'd been maneuvered. At first he'd been furious, but Hartley was as smooth as they came, and Sean had never lived as he was living now.

Meals were delivered, beds were made, his clothes, finer than those at Buck's, were always kept washed and pressed—he had everything but the red carpet. It didn't even seem to matter that Sean was a bodyguard and not the man with the money; he was treated like a king.

The job had very few drawbacks—none at all, if Sean could keep his conscience silenced. It wasn't the easiest thing when Hartley would get roaring drunk and pass out, leaving Sean to put him to bed. And it was harder still when Hartley brought girls up to his room, only to have them wait until Hartley was asleep before they paid a visit to Sean. He never let them stay, but there were times when he wondered why.

Sean convinced himself that on the whole, it was a good life. It even included travel. Hartley had informed him just the day before that they would be leaving Tulare today. He hadn't said exactly where they were going, and almost before Sean could question him, he found himself on horseback, following his employer out of town.

The weeks to follow were spent in a dusty haze. Gone were the fancy hotel rooms and room service.

When Sean finally questioned his employer, Hartley responded, "It's time to go back to work."

Sean wondered at his own stupidity in thinking the luxury would last forever. They could only live high until the money ran out, and then Hartley was back at his thieving game. He didn't care from whom he stole, just so long as the victim was outside of Tulare. They rode into some towns in the dead of night, and Sean knew if he'd been questioned he would not have been able to tell anyone where he had been.

He also realized with sobering clarity that even though he was not a part of the robberies, his presence made him an accessory. There were times when he asked himself why he stayed, especially when he stood waiting in dark alleys and back streets for Hartley to appear. It never took more than a few minutes to remind himself, however, that he had been the one to walk away from Santa Rosa and his family. With that in mind and convincing himself they wanted nothing more to do with him, he knew he had no place else to go. He stayed on.

Weeks passed. Thanksgiving came and went and still they were on the road. Christmas passed, as did Sean's nineteenth birthday, with little or no notice. Finally, after an especially profitable night, Hartley stole some supplies, loaded them on Sean's horse, sat a comely barmaid he'd been taken with onto his own mount and headed them up into the foothills outside of Visalia.

When Sean woke, fully dressed and in an unmade bed, he realized how long and exhausting their midnight ride had been. Once again he had no idea where he was. He emerged from his bedroom to a spacious, if rundown cabin. The view out the dirty windows was glorious, and not bothering to close the door behind him, Sean went outside. Beauty notwithstanding, Sean was already feeling restless, and was glad when Hartley joined him.

"You're up early," the smaller man commented as he rolled and lit a cigarette.

"What are we doing here?" Sean came directly to the point.

"It is necessary, Sean, to lay low for a time. I have a few more jobs to do, but they will take some planning."

"I don't care to be stuck up here with nothing to do."

"But there is plenty to do. There is money to count, food to eat, beds to sleep in, and of course, there is Anita."

Sean gave him a blank look. "No, thank you."

Hartley had been looking forward to a rest, but he could see that Sean was not going to stand for it. He was a little surprised to find that he liked Sean enough to alter his plans. Sean was one of the best men he'd ever ridden with; his sharp eyes and usually calm ways were a valuable asset. There was much about him that remained a mystery, but Hartley was sure they'd be together for a long time, plenty of time to someday learn it all.

Hartley returned to the cabin without a word, and told Anita to start breakfast. Sean, telling himself to relax, let the matter drop for the time. Just 24 hours later he was calling himself a fool for doing so. He woke and found that Hartley had ridden out, leaving him and Anita alone.

five

Sean was in a tower rage as he packed his saddlebags and gear. He hoped to never see Hartley again, because if he did, he was going to strangle him. The woman at the house watched in surprise as he took supplies from the kitchen, leaving disaster in his wake. She then watched from the front door as he rode away from the cabin without a word. Had Sean cared to put his emotions aside, he'd have noticed her calm, and understood that Hartley hadn't left for good, and was, in fact, planning to return as soon as possible.

As it was, Sean returned also. Try as he might, he could not find his way out of the hills. It seemed that each trail he found became impassable within several miles of the cabin. Angry and frustrated, he returned late at night, now wishing Hartley was on hand so he could choke the life out of the man. He dropped on his bed, fully clothed and asking himself how he'd come to be in this place. At last he fell into a restless sleep.

In the morning Sean's mood had not improved. Anita had put some breakfast on the table, but was nowhere to be found. This was fine with Sean, who sat down and ate like he'd not had a meal in weeks, still asking himself why he'd let himself be suckered in by Hartley.

Having lost his razor, he hadn't shaved since they'd left Tulare, but that didn't stop him from wanting to be clean. "I can hardly stand myself," he grumbled as he stripped to the waist after his meal and scrubbed up at the basin that stood next to the cabin's only door.

He was just finishing his wash, changing into the last of his clean clothes, when two riders came into the yard, Hartley and another man. Sean was out the door and reaching for Hartley before he could dismount. He yanked the smaller man from the saddle and held him in the air by the front of his vest.

"I will not be toyed with," his voice sent a chill down Hartley's spine, and he actually smelled fear, thinking Sean was about to kill him. "I am not your slave. Now you can get back in that saddle and lead me out of these hills, or I'm going to put a bullet through you."

Sean dropped a gasping Hartley in a heap at his feet and strode back into the house to collect his gear. Hartley followed, and for the first time Sean saw him lose his perfect composure.

"I'm sorry, Sean. Listen to me," the older man begged. "I never dreamed you wouldn't know I was coming back. I left Anita. Didn't she tell you we needed another man? I didn't think you'd want to come. Honestly, Sean, I was just thinking of you. You're my partner, Sean—I wouldn't do anything to hurt you."

This last sentence was the only one to arrest Sean's attention. Hartley had never called him a partner before, and for some reason the word had a calming effect on him. Hartley, smooth as a snake-oil salesman, saw that he'd penetrated Sean's anger. In the blink of an eye he had everyone gathered around the table, talking to them and including them in his plans as though they'd been friends for years.

It took Sean the better part of the next 15 minutes to fully understand that Hartley was planning something bigger this time. The man who had come with him, Rico by name, was a bit dim, but seemed all for the plan.

"You're going to rob a bank." Anita too, had been slow on the uptake, and Hartley patted her cheek when she understood.

"I thought we were going to break into someone's house," Rico admitted, sounding just a bit unsure.

"How about you, Sean, did you understand?"

"Only just. Have you done this before—robbed a bank?

"Never in Visalia, but elsewhere." Hartley spoke with casual ease. "There's nothing to it, Sean; you'll see. And if there is some danger, we're talking about thousands of dollars here—well worth the risk."

"Who gets the money?" Anita wanted to know, catching Hartley's excitement.

"We all do," Hartley told her with a smile.

Sean knew that this was a now-or-never point in his life. His father's face suddenly sprang into his head, and Sean wondered where he was. *It doesn't matter*, he thought after just a moment. *He doesn't want to see me anyway.*

In an effort to hide the pain Sean bent low over the bank plan now laid out on the table. "Count me in" was all he said before everyone fell quiet and allowed Hartley to explain.

six

Santa Rosa, California

Rigg was exhausted, but sleep would not come. He was sure this stemmed from the fact that his wife was not in bed with him. He rolled onto his side to better see the woman who sat in the rocking chair, her silhouette illuminated by the moonlight flooding through the window.

Katie had been sitting motionless for more than an hour. She knew she would never be able to get out of bed in the morning if she didn't lie down and get some rest soon, but her heart was so heavy with thoughts of her brother, Sean, that sleep seemed hours away.

How long had it been since they had seen him? Nearly two years—Molly had been an infant. Nearly two years since Aunt Maureen had written, beside herself that he had gone off on his own. They had been forced to accept Sean's decision, but there had been times when it had been close to torture to sit and wonder where he might be.

So why, tonight of all nights, was he so heavy on her heart? Every day she thought of him, and prayed that God would guide his path and someday bring him home, but tonight was different; tonight there was an urgency in her thoughts. Something was happening this night, and Kaitlin knew she had to pray.

She also knew that if Sean had been in the room, she would have held onto him with all her strength to keep him from . . . to keep him from what, she was not sure. But somehow Kate was certain that Sean needed protection of some type at that very moment. Not that he would have welcomed her interference in his life. He had wanted as little to do with her at 16 and 17 as any teen could. He hadn't wanted advice or even affection, from her or anyone else.

Nineteen and a half now, Kate thought to herself. Surely he would feel some different.

Rigg stirred in the bed when someone knocked on the bedroom door. Kate, not wanting him to be disturbed, started to rise, but Rigg was already to the door. He opened it and found Marcail, now 14, waiting outside in her gown and robe. Rigg, not understanding why Kate was awake, also wondered at the fact Marcail wasn't sound asleep.

Rigg stepped back and allowed her to see Kate at the window. She moved forward and stopped beside the rocking chair, letting Kate see her face in the moonlight.

"I can't sleep."

"No," Kaitlin spoke softly, "I can't either. Are you worried about Sean?"

Marcail nodded, misery written all over her young face. "Where is he, Katie?"

"I wish I knew."

"I can't get him out of my mind."

"I can't either."

"Do you think he's in trouble?"

This time it was Katie's turn to nod. "We've got to pray, Marc. God knows all about this, and we're going to give it to Him right now."

Both girls bowed their heads. As sisters, each in her own way, they petitioned God on behalf of their brother.

Marcail, really still just a girl, asked God to keep Sean safe, and to bring him back to Santa Rosa right away so they would know he was all right.

Kaitlin, a mother, prayed differently. She prayed that Sean would make wise choices and seek God's will above his own. She also prayed that God would be glorified in Sean's life, even if it meant her beloved brother would have to know a season of pain.

seven

Visalia, California

We *all experience seasons, Sean. They're not the predictable seasons, such as winter and summer, but the unpredictable seasons that come into our lives. I'm talking about times of loneliness or grief, or seasons of joy and peacefulness. But no matter what the weather in our hearts, Sean, we've got to keep our eyes on God.*

Why Katie's words of long ago would come to Sean so strongly at that instant was beyond him. He felt another trickle of sweat run from his temple down into his beard, but still he didn't move. How he had gotten himself into such a mess, he couldn't for the moment remember. But then he heard the low whistle—the signal—and there was no more time for thought.

As Sean rushed through the rear doorway of the bank, he nearly stumbled over a body. Stopping dead in his tracks, he felt a sudden jolt as Rico, the man behind, ran into him.

"What are you doing?" Rico sounded as breathless as Sean felt, and Sean turned to find his features in the darkness.

"Nobody said anything about killing."

"He's not dead you idiot, now get over here with those sacks!"

These words were ground out by Hartley from his place by the safe, and the two young bank robbers rushed forward to comply. Sean had never heard Hartley sound so tense. Suddenly the enormity of what they were about to do froze Sean in his tracks.

"Get behind something, it's almost ready to blow."

These words were enough to propel Sean into action. He dove for cover just as the entire world seemed to explode. The next minutes were a blur to Sean as he choked on the smoke and tried to be in all six of the places he was being commanded.

He froze again when he heard shots outside, and felt completely rattled as a vision of being shot raced through his mind. Still stunned, he watched in fascination as his companions ran out the back, their arms full of sacks hastily stuffed with United States currency.

"*Donovan!*"

Not even the furious shouting of his name could compel his feet forward; by the time Sean reacted, it was too late. He spun around as men with guns came pouring in the front door. He turned and moved after Hartley and Rico, but he hadn't gone two steps when another man came through the back door with a gun. Sean listened in stunned disbelief as the men yelled that Sean's partners had escaped.

Sean felt numb. He was barely aware of the man who laid hands on him until he gave a cruel yank to Sean's arms. Now painfully alert as his hands were being cuffed behind his back, Sean started as a face suddenly pressed close to his own and snarled in a voice full of hate, "If he's dead, you'll hang."

"He'll hang either way if I have anything to say about it."

Sean's confused mind barely registered this last comment as he was *escorted* to the door. He was surprised at the number of people on the streets, but then remembered the deafening sound of the explosion and wondered how in the world they had believed they could get away with such a robbery.

The back wall of the jail cell was the only obstacle that kept Sean from hitting the floor as he was pushed violently past the bars. The clanging of the door was like the sound of a death knell in his ears.

Squinting through the gloom of the small cell, Sean saw a cot. He sat down with his hands still tied and leaned slowly back against the wall. If they left his hands tied until morning he was certain to be disgraced as the need to relieve himself was pressing in stronger with every passing moment. That, along with the receding fear, caused Sean's anger to return. He was working himself into a fine rage, telling himself he was going to kill Hartley as soon as he was released, when he heard voices in the outer room.

"It's what he deserves I tell you! This waiting is utter foolishness."

"Yet we will wait for Judge Harrison, and I'm telling *you*, you'll have to go past me to get to the prisoner."

"Be reasonable, Duncan. Why wait two whole days and have the trouble of feeding and watching him?"

There was no reply to that question, and Sean realized that every muscle in his body was as taut as a well-strung bow. He waited in the dark silence, and after a few more minutes he thought he heard people leaving.

He must have been right because his jailer returned to the cell holding a lamp and a shotgun. He was with another man, and this man let himself into the cell to remove Sean's bonds. Sean was more than a little aware of the way the barrel of the shotgun never wavered from his chest. If he could have spoken, he would have told the men he couldn't run. His legs would never hold him.

They didn't speak to Sean or to each other, but before the men left the cell they stared at Sean for a few intense seconds. His fear returned fullscale at having these two men staring at him. Knowing he was completely at their mercy was even more frightening than when the safe blew.

If the light had been better, Sean might have noticed that the older man's look was regretful, not cruel.

□ □ □

"He's nothing but a kid." The deep voice was soft, contemplative.

"How could you tell under all that hair?"

"His eyes. Clear as glass and angry, but scared out of his wits."

The deputy only nodded, sure that Sheriff Lucas Duncan, "Duncan" to all, was right. He usually was.

"Want me to stay the night?"

"No. I'm restless as it is, but stop and let Lora know that I'm all right and ask her to bring breakfast for two."

"Right. I'm off."

An hour passed before Duncan moved again. He'd been deep in thought and knew that his hunch had been right: There would be little if any sleep for him tonight. Had he gone home, he'd have tossed and turned for hours, disturbing Lora.

Duncan pushed away from his desk then, the chair creaking in protest. He had planned to question the boy at daybreak, but if he was as restless as the sheriff, now was as good a time as any.

Duncan was surprised to find his prisoner asleep. He was stretched out on his back, one arm thrown over his eyes. Duncan let his eyes run the length of him. He was big. He covered the cot and then some. It was easy to see why Hartley picked him; his size alone could be intimidating.

But Duncan wasn't fooled. He guessed him to be somewhere around 20 and as wet behind the ears as they came. And at 54, Duncan had seen more than a few prisoners come and go.

He walked back to his desk, sat down, and propped his feet on the flat surface. After laying his gun across his stomach, he tipped his hat forward and his chair back. He caught about an hour's sleep before his wife came in with breakfast and a smile.

eight

Lora Duncan set her tray on the desk and went immediately to kiss her husband. His arms came around her plump figure as Lora looked anxiously into his eyes. He was exhausted.

"Hartley?"

"He was behind it, but he's not in the cell."

Lora nodded and moved to unload her husband's breakfast. She left the prisoner's food on the tray and followed Duncan to the cell. She hung back slightly until he signaled her forward, and then entered the cell and put the tray on the floor. She didn't linger within, but once outside took a moment to look at the man sitting silently on the cot. He was watching her, and Lora was immediately struck by his youth.

"I'll be coming back to talk to you as soon as I eat."

Lora barely heard her husband's words to the man before she was gently ushered back to the desk.

"He's young and trying to hide it behind his anger," she whispered with tears in her eyes.

"Yes, he is young, and I think I'd better warn you, they plan to make an example out of him."

Duncan's voice was equally soft, and he watched with pain as a shudder ran over his wife's frame. He hated to see her upset, but it was better that she know now than on the day the kid swung from a rope.

Lora had brought along a pot of coffee and joined Duncan as he ate. They talked of nothing in particular, and as soon as Duncan was finished he urged her to go home.

"What if he didn't like the food? I could always fix him something else."

Duncan looked at her with tender eyes, but the set of his mouth told her that no one was going to baby this prisoner. Lora realized he needed to be as stern with himself as he was with her. She left without an argument.

❑ ❑ ❑

Sean told himself that he wouldn't be able to eat a thing, but one taste of the eggs and bacon on the plate, and the food disappeared like magic. He was sitting back on the cot, the tray still beside him, when Duncan came back.

He unlocked the cell door and signaled Sean out with his gun. Once by the desk Duncan handcuffed one of Sean's wrists and closed the other cuff around a ring on the wall.

"Have a seat." The older man directed him to the chair that sat beneath the ring. It wasn't the most comfortable position, but Sean took little notice.

He watched the sheriff take a seat behind the desk and draw some papers out of a drawer.

"What's your name?"

It was the first of many questions, including everything Sean knew about the robbery and those involved. It occurred to Sean that this man might be his ticket out of here, so he didn't lie or try to protect his accomplices.

He was quiet and somewhat respectful, but his anger at Hartley made him feel like a kettle on the verge of a boilover.

After an hour's worth of questioning about Hartley, the cabin, and the robbery, Duncan asked where Sean was from.

"Santa Rosa."

"North of San Francisco, right?"

"Yes, sir."

The men stared at each other for the space of a few heartbeats.

"Where are your folks, son?"

Not even his anger could hide the pain in the younger man's eyes as he answered. "My mother is dead and last I knew, my father," Sean's jaw tightened on the word, "was in Hawaii."

Duncan didn't reply to this right away. Sean was unaware of how swiftly the other man's mind was moving. *Angry or not, this kid knows he's done wrong, regrets it, and knows he's going to have to be punished.* The thought startled Duncan.

"How'd you meet Hartley?"

"We met in Tulare. He sort of appeared out of nowhere and offered me a job. I was tired and broke and he bought me supper. Then we just sort of struck out together. How did you know it was Hartley?"

"His style never varies. Middle of the night, dynamite, young men as accomplices."

"He's robbed this bank before?" Sean was shocked.

"Three times," the sheriff replied dryly.

What a fool he'd been to think that Hartley had been honest with him about anything. He'd certainly left him fast enough when the bullets started to fly.

"This is a reasonable time to warn you that you probably don't have a chance."

"What do you mean?"

"Only that the owner of the bank is tired of the rob-beries and believes that if they make an example of you, Hartley will never be back. You see, he waits long enough between robberies to make everyone relax. Just about the time Witt pulls his night guards off duty, or has just one, Hartley hits again."

Sean assumed that Witt was the banker. He also figured out that he had been the man who had not wanted to wait last night. *Wait for what?* Sean had asked himself. Now he knew they had been speaking of his hanging. Suddenly Sean wished he hadn't eaten any breakfast.

Duncan had been correct in assuming that Sean had resigned himself to spending some time in jail, but Sean had never considered being hanged. His calmness abruptly disappeared, and the faces of his sisters sprang into his mind. What would Kate and Marcail say? Would they ever even know?

Sean stood, his panicked heart hammering the walls of his chest before he looked down at his cuffed wrist. Duncan's heart turned over at the look of terror that passed over his prisoner's eyes. He then watched in fascination as the young man visibly worked at calming himself. Sean sat back down and swallowed with diffi-culty, but when he spoke, his voice was even.

"I have a sister in Santa Rosa. If I give you her address will you contact her after—"

"Let's not rush things," Duncan told him softly. "I just wanted to warn you. If and when I need to contact your family, I'll get the address then."

Sean nodded and realized he had an awful headache. Duncan returned him to the cell, removed the breakfast tray, and left him alone.

A dog barked outside the window, and an old woman was screeching at some kids in the street. Sean heard none of it. He fell asleep trying to pray—something he hadn't done for well over two years.

❑ ❑ ❑

When Sean woke it was midmorning. He immediately remembered Duncan's words and thought of his own hanging. He realized that his head felt better, and his anger was gone, but his heart still thundered within him like that of a trapped bird. *Trapped*. A very fitting word for a man in a cell, and even though he wanted to blame Hartley, he couldn't. It was time to face the fact that he had no one to blame but himself.

Suddenly Hartley's words from the cabin as they bent over the plan of the bank came rushing back to Sean. "Nothing to it, Sean, you'll see." Sean's throat emitted a hoarse, humorless laugh.

"You've been a fool, Sean Donovan," he whispered. "And you're going to pay for that foolishness with your life."

Sean rolled over to his stomach on the narrow cot and let the tears flow. At the same time he wept, Sean once again began to pray. He surrendered his heart to God, with all its anger and bitterness, for the first time since his mother died.

nine

Two days later Sean was handcuffed and led to the courthouse. The small building was packed and stifling. Sean's mouth had never been so dry, and he longingly eyed the pitcher of water sitting on the judge's table.

Judge Thomas Harrison entered, going straight to his chair. Sean was surprised by his appearance, for he was very small in stature, not even up to Sean's shoulder. The most remarkable feature about him was his full beard; it nearly obscured his face.

The next two hours would forever live in Sean's mind. The sheriff gave a full report on all Sean had told him, including his behavior as a prisoner, his background, and the way Hartley had used naive young men in the past to rob banks with him.

Franklin Witt was not so benevolent. He proclaimed that Sean was no better than a two-bit thief, and that the country was better off without such vermin. He reminded the court that one of his guards had been hit on the head and could have been killed. After this he announced, in a voice heard by all, that Sean Donovan should die.

"Might I remind you," Witt nearly shouted, "that this will continue to happen? And when Hartley and his gang are done with the bank, they'll start on our homes. Are you going to set this man free to rob again?" Witt was in his element, and he was determined to convince the judge that Sean needed to hang.

Franklin Witt was a man in his forties with a full head of gray hair and a distinguished air of authority about him that captured everyone's attention. He took great pride in his position as town banker, and even greater pride at the amount of property he owned.

When it came to his business dealings, some said there was a demon behind his smile. He was more than willing to loan money, but if a mortgage or rent payment was overdue, he was merciless. It was said that he had a special book in his pocket where he kept track of how many homes and properties he had repossessed since coming to town five years ago. The joke around town was that whenever Franklin Witt was smiling, he must have been reading in his little black book.

"All right, Witt, I've heard enough. Do you have anything else, Duncan?"

"He's already had his say!"

The judge stared Witt back down into his chair and Duncan stood.

"Only this, judge. Sean needs to pay for the crime he's committed, but not with his life."

Witt came out of his chair once again, but one look from the judge and he kept his mouth shut. Judge Harrison's eyes swung from Witt to Duncan, and finally to Sean. The regret Sean saw in those eyes made his heart pound.

"The prisoner will stand."

Sean complied.

"You're a man, Sean Donovan," the judge began. "No one forced you to rob that bank. As much as I grieve this course of action, this court sentences you to death."

The noise of the court was deafening with protests and cheers alike. *It really is a shame,* the judge thought to himself, *that this young man has to be the example. But Witt is right, it'll continue to happen unless I step in and put a stop to it.* None of the judge's feelings showed on his face as he held Sean's eyes with his own. He spoke when the room quieted.

"The building of the gallows will commence immediately and tomorrow afternoon, at 4:30, Sean Donovan will be hanged by the neck until dead. This court is adjourned."

Duncan caught Sean as his legs began to buckle beneath him. "Steady, son." The softly whispered words were just enough to keep Sean upright. Knowing that someone in this room cared for him was all he needed. The Lord had given him that much, and for that he was thankful.

□ □ □

"Thomas is coming for supper," Duncan told his wife as he came in the kitchen door.

"Good. I made extra, hoping you would ask him." Lora paused and studied her husband's face. She didn't need to ask what the verdict had been for his young prisoner; it was written all over his face.

The ladies from the church had been over that day, and they'd all taken time from their quilting to pray. Most had prayed for the prisoner and the judge's decision, but Lora had remembered her husband. She had prayed for his peace of mind, as well as strength to do his job, even if the worst happened and Duncan would be called upon to hang a man.

"Are you all right?" She asked softly when Duncan sat at the table.

"Yeah. It's going to be rough, but I'm trusting the Lord."

Lora moved away from the stove and put her arms around him. Duncan's eyes slid shut at the feel and smell of her. She was stability when his world felt shattered. She was logical when his emotional strength was at an end. Without a doubt, she was God's most precious gift to him.

He told her as much, and then they took time to pray before supper. Duncan asked God to sustain Sean in the hours to come. Lora asked the same for Duncan, wishing all the while that her husband could be spared from such a task but never dreaming that it could really happen.

❑ ❑ ❑

"You've done it again haven't you, Lucas?"

The sheriff didn't answer the judge. He took the bowl of potatoes Lora was passing him and served himself. The judge was right—he had done it again. He had grown overly compassionate in his job. It had never made him err in judgment, but it made the inevitable, such as Sean's hanging, feel like a knife in his side.

"I'm staying for the hanging."

Duncan looked at him in surprise. The implication was clear, and he resented it.

"I can handle it."

"I know you can, but I've decided to stay and spare you."

Duncan felt badly for his presumption. Praising God that Duncan would not have to pull that handle, Lora swallowed hard against a sudden rush of tears.

"Thanks, Tom." Duncan said the words aloud; Lora said them in her heart.

Nothing more was said on the subject, and when the meal was finished the men left. Duncan told Lora that he would be home around midmorning. Judge Harrison walked with Duncan as far as the hotel where the men bid each other goodnight.

Duncan's deputy had been expecting him, and other than Sean's not eating his supper, he had nothing to report. Duncan knew how easy it would be to try to coax Sean into eating, but given the same circumstances, he knew he himself would not want to be patronized.

He picked up an extra chair and carried it down to the front of Sean's cell. After turning it around, he sat astride it and looked at his prisoner where he sat on the cot.

"I'm sorry about today, Sean. I prayed it would be different." These words and the actions of the past two days told Sean that the man across from him was a fellow believer in Christ.

"I did too, but I know that since it wasn't, that's the way it's supposed to be."

All of Duncan's suspicions were confirmed. "How did you get this far from God, Sean?"

"It didn't happen overnight," Sean admitted quietly. "I fought Him every step of the way; in fact I fought Him so much that I was certain He had given up on me. I found out today that He hadn't given up at all." Considering that Sean had been sentenced to hang, most people wouldn't have been able to make any sense of his statement, but Duncan understood.

"Want to tell me about it?" Duncan asked quietly.

"It's a long story."

"I've got all night."

Sean stared at the older man for just a moment, and then began to speak in a reminiscent voice, not about all he'd been thinking on that day, but further back, back to his childhood in Hawaii.

"I was born in Hawaii where my parents were missionaries. I went to school there and of course church, and I really believed I'd live there forever. It was my world.

"Then on my sister's twentieth birthday, when I was 14, my father announced that we would be sailing to California for a rest and family vacation. I'd never known such a mixture of fear and happiness. I'd also never really known the definition of the word seasick.

"I prayed for death on that trip. My stomach heaved until it was empty and then heaved some more." Sean's whole body shuddered with the memory. "I was certain I would be dead by the time we arrived in San Francisco. That's where my aunt lives. We moved in with her, and then my parents revealed the real reason we'd left Hawaii. My mother was ill. She was diagnosed with tuberculosis. It was only a matter of weeks and she was gone.

"Father felt burdened to return to the islands and gather our things." A slight tone of anger entered Sean's voice. "We were to stay with Aunt Maureen, and we did, but then my cousin Percy came home."

Questions came to Duncan's mind as Sean talked, but now that Sean had begun, he stayed silent and sensitive to the young man's need to tell his story.

"I swear I could have killed him when I walked in and saw him with his arms around my sister. Kaitlin had tried to warn me, but I thought she was overreacting." Sean took a deep breath as he remembered the pain he felt over Percy's actions and his father's absence. But then Rigg's face came to mind.

"She has a good husband now. He loves her and their little girls. Oh," Sean realized he hadn't explained. "It was after we moved to Santa Rosa that she met Rigg. When Kate felt that we couldn't stay in San Francisco any longer because of Percy's advances, we took the stage north and she got a job teaching school.

"Moving without being able to talk it over with Father was the hardest thing we'd ever done. We were all right though, and I believed my father would come any time, but he didn't. Weeks went by before we heard from him, and then his letter said he was needed in the islands and wanted to stay.

"It was worse in some ways than when Mother died, because we waited in anticipation of each letter, only to be disappointed. My heart grew more bitter with each passing month. When he'd been gone for two Christmases in a row, I felt so full of pent-up anger I thought I would explode.

"I finally left Santa Rosa the summer I was 17. It wasn't long before I started telling myself I would never go back. I'd also been telling myself for two years that if my father could desert me then my God probably could as well. So I stopped trying to pray, certain there was no one listening.

"And then today, when you cared enough to hold me on my feet, I knew I'd been wrong. He'd been there all along, waiting to help me with the pain of loss and separation. It's easy to say this now that I know how close my death is," Sean hesitated and tears filled his dark eyes, "but I would serve God with my whole heart if I had another chance."

Duncan wanted to say something but couldn't swallow around the lump in his throat.

"Thanks for coming back and talking to me. It makes things a little easier. Will you take that address now?"

Duncan nodded and went for some paper. When he returned, Sean's voice shook as he gave Kaitlin's full name and address.

"Try to get some sleep, Sean."

"I will, and please tell my sisters that I love them and that I love Father too."

Duncan's throat closed again, and he waited until the younger man lay down before taking the piece of paper to his desk. He sat unseeing for a long time, the paper clutched in his fingers.

When he did open a bottom drawer in the desk to file the paper, he hesitated. It was a mess inside. His file system left much to be desired.

He put the address in his breast pocket for safekeeping and reached again to shut the drawer. Something stopped him, however, something he hadn't thought about in years.

Like a man in a dream he reached into the drawer time and again until the contents were emptied onto his desk. The document was hazy in his mind, but he was sure it must be there. Duncan looked at the mass of papers on the desktop and wondered where to start.

His hesitation lasted only a moment before he remembered that 4:30 the next afternoon was less than 17 hours away. With that thought in mind, he began to read.

ten

"Where did you find this?"

"I've been searching my papers all night. Is it any good?"

Judge Harrison didn't answer, but continued to study the document in his hand. Finally he said, "I'd forgotten all about this law."

"I had too. Is it still legal?"

"Oh, yes," the petite man assured him calmly.

"Will you read it?"

"I'll read it, Lucas," he said as he looked the taller man in the eye, "but you must know that the possibility of a response—"

"I don't know anything, Tom, except that you've *got* to read that proclamation," Duncan cut him off. "I know it's a shot in the dark, but I'm trusting God in that darkness. I don't know how and I don't know who—I just know you've got to read that paper."

The judge studied the sheriff's face for a long moment. He had always respected Duncan's faith in God. "I'll read it Duncan; for what it's worth, I'll read it."

❏ ❏ ❏

It was a sobering experience for Sean to hear the

54

hammers pounding nails to form the gallows where he would meet his death. Sean's window did not look out onto the building site, but as the sun passed its midpoint in the sky, a shadow was cast across the ground, giving a perfect outline of the tall structure that would see his execution.

Sean's hand rose involuntarily to his throat as he lay down on the cot. "I know Your arms are waiting to hold me on the other side, Lord, but the thought of that rope around my neck terrifies me."

The words were whispered, and tears stung Sean's eyes. "Please help me to be strong. I don't know if I've ever given You the glory for anything, but I want to now."

And such were Sean's prayers through the long afternoon. Since he knew his system would hold nothing, he hadn't eaten a thing since before the trial. He was, in a sense, fasting and praying, and God's immeasurable peace had settled upon him. Duncan had come and talked to him again that morning and then prayed aloud, thanking God for the opportunity to know Sean. It had almost been the younger man's undoing.

Knowing that Duncan would write a kind letter to his family, Sean praised God. He tried to push the faces of his sisters and his nieces from his mind, but it did no good. He adored his nieces, and the thought of never seeing them again brought a torrent of tears.

Having dozed off before Duncan came to get him, Sean shook his head to clear his mind and held his wrists behind his back for cuffing.

Sean's heart, which had been beating at normal speed, began to pound when he saw the crowd around the scaffolding. It had never occurred to him that people would care to witness such a gruesome spectacle, but there was indeed quite a crowd gathered, and it was painful to have to walk through the midst of them to his death.

The walk up the steps of the scaffold was the longest of Sean's life. He was momentarily surprised to see the judge waiting for him on the platform, but a second later he stepped onto the trapdoor and felt the rope tighten around his neck and all other thoughts vanished.

The sun was in Sean's face, and not wishing to see the faces in the crowd, he welcomed the excuse to close his eyes. The noises around him and the feel of the rope as it scraped the tender skin of his neck were all he could take.

"It's been recently brought to my attention that a document needs to be read at this hanging. For some of you it will be new. For others, it'll jog your memory from many years ago. But either way I assure you, it is legal and I will hear no discussion to the contrary."

The judge cleared his throat and began to read. "As official of this legal hanging in the State of California, in the County of Tulare, I hereby proclaim that for the offense of bank robbery, Sean Donovan will be hanged by the neck until dead. *Unless*, in said case, a woman of good standing in the community, that is, not being a woman of ill repute, a child beater, or an adulteress, will hereby step forward and claim said prisoner to be her lawfully wedded spouse from this day forward."

The announcement was met with gasps of shock and outrage from the throng. An ominous silence followed.

"Now, I should explain a little further, without having to read the whole thing, that this would not apply to the offense of murder. And since I know I've taken you all by surprise, I'll read it one more time."

The judge did as he said without looking anywhere but at the paper. If he had he would have seen the condemned man staring at him, his eyes nearly popping out of his head.

Sean would have sworn that nothing but the sight of his Savior would have been able to pry open his eyes, but when the judge began reading the document, his eyes flew open and he swiveled his head as best he could to look at the man next to him.

The judge finished reading a second later, and Sean was still so busy staring at him that he didn't hear a woman calling from the crowd. Murmurs of "Charlie" came to his ears, but the name didn't really register.

Sean watched Duncan's face in disbelief as the sheriff loosened the knot and lifted the rope from his neck. Spots danced before his eyes.

"Don't pass out now, Sean. Charlie has just agreed to marry you."

Sean's eyes went from the grinning sheriff to the judge, who was staring down the steps of the scaffold to a woman standing below. Sean followed his gaze and saw black spots again. With Duncan's hand gripping his arm, he was brought back to his senses just as the judge addressed him.

"Well, son, it seems there's been a change in the plans. Can you stay on your feet long enough to be married?"

eleven

Duncan stared down at the redheaded woman in front of him and tried not to smile. Charlotte Cooper, "Charlie" to the entire town, was the hardest working woman in the area. Deceptively attractive under her dusty clothes, Charlie did a good job of hiding her beauty beneath the hat she wore, the brim of which was always stubbornly pulled down to her brows.

Charlie and Duncan were alone in the judge's chambers where she had just become Mrs. Patrick Sean Donovan III. She didn't appear overjoyed, and Duncan was thankful that they had tied the knot before she could change her mind. He didn't by any means believe this was a match made in heaven, but he *did* believe that if God had brought Sean this far, He would see him the rest of the way.

"I think he'll be just fine, Charlie," Duncan told her after Sean went to her wagon with his deputy.

"He'd better be, Duncan," she told him seriously, wondering again at the impulse that now had her married. "Because if he makes one move out of line, I'll bring him back here and you can just go right ahead and hang him higher than Haman."

Duncan did smile then, not believing for a second that she was as indifferent as she sounded. His smile only caused Charlie to frown.

"What are you grinning about?" she growled at him.

Duncan didn't answer, and Charlie shook her head and exited the courthouse.

Sean was waiting patiently where he had been directed. He watched his wife approach and felt a state of shock settle over him. His wife. He was married! And to an absolute stranger!

Charlie stopped in front of him and looked out under the battered hat. Her eyes were serious, and Sean wondered what she was thinking.

"I hope you're not afraid of hard work," she muttered as she hitched her skirt enough to climb into the wagon unassisted. "You can sit in the back."

Sean did as he was told, careful not to sit on the supplies neatly stacked in the rear of the wagon. Duncan stepped to the sideboard and spoke softly.

"I wanted to warn you about the paper I'd found, Sean, but I was afraid of getting your hopes up. Charlie will do right by you. Just follow the rules and you'll be fine." They shook hands, and Duncan told the still-speechless Sean that the door to his office was always open.

A moment later the wagon was moving down the street. Sean sat still as they went into the next block. No more than 30 seconds had passed before the wagon pulled straight into the livery. The sign above the door read "COOPER'S LIVERY" in large, faded letters.

The horse and wagon stopped inside the sturdy-looking building. Sean jumped out of the back as soon as the wagon halted and without forethought, moved to help his wife. Charlie stared at the hand extended to her and then at the owner. Sean's hand dropped, and he stepped back and watched as she jumped to the ground.

Her manner was plainly suspicious, and Sean told himself he was going to have to watch his step. Feeling rather helpless, he stood back as Charlie stabled her horse and began to rub him down.

"You don't need to unload that wagon until tomorrow, so just push it into the big stall on the end." It was a command and Sean was swift to do her bidding. He stood just outside the stall once the wagon was in place, waiting for his next orders. The livery in which he stood was clean, spacious, and well supplied. There were horses in five other stalls, and from where he stood, Sean thought he could see another wagon and two buggies.

When Charlie finished with the horse, she walked to the front of the livery and pulled the double doors shut. There were double doors at the back also, but they were already closed and Sean watched as she headed toward another small door. She hesitated on the threshold.

"I don't suppose you know an anvil from a saddle, but my blacksmith just walked out on me. I'm finished here for the night, and my supper will be coming. You can start work in the morning." Sean stood still as he listened to his wife, unsure if he should tell her he was an experienced blacksmith. While he was still debating whether or not to speak, Charlie left without another word.

She walked with swift purpose to the door of her house, not turning to look behind her until her hand was reaching for the handle.

"Now where in the world is he?" Charlie muttered to herself when she saw that Sean had not followed her. She stood still and gave a small sigh, wondering once again why she had married him. Charlie told herself quickly it was because of his size. A man that big would be worth hours of work in a livery, as soon as she taught him how to smith.

She waited a second longer, hoping he would appear in the livery doorway, but it was not to be. Suddenly she felt very suspicious. With a mixture of fear and anger, Charlie moved back toward the livery.

❑ ❑ ❑

Sean glanced around at his new home and wondered in which stall he should bed down. It was early yet, but if he slept he might not notice how empty his stomach was. He stood for a moment, his hand on the tender area of his throat. His eyes slid shut as he once again felt the rope.

"Thank you, Lord," Sean whispered, still staggered by the fact that he was alive. He felt down his own arms and then to his legs before the vision of himself hanging from a rope sprang into his mind. His palms became damp, and he shook his head to dispel the image before beginning to walk along the stalls, desperate for something to distract his mind.

The tack wall caught and held his interest. He was immediately impressed with the quality of halters, bridles, and saddles. He stood looking them over when his wife's suspicious voice made him snatch his cap off and turn to face her.

"Is there some problem?"

"No ma'am." Sean noticed she was frowning as she had been when she exited the courthouse.

"Then why didn't you follow me?"

"I assumed you wanted me to bunk out here."

Something in his voice, as well as the way he held his

cap in both hands, tempered Charlie's voice as she replied.

"Your room is in the house." She watched him replace his cap and move carefully toward her. Her anger evaporated, and she suddenly felt a little sorry for him. After all, he was to have been executed today. But by the time Sean was close enough to see her face, she'd carefully hidden this emotion.

"Come on," she said and once again headed outside. Sean followed her this time and saw that she was leading him to a small house some 50 feet behind the livery.

Stepping through the front doorway Sean found himself in the kitchen, but he wasn't given any time to inspect his new home. "This way's your room."

Charlie led him down a short hallway where Sean saw two doors. One door was straight in front of him and one was on the left side of the hall. Charlie opened the door on the left.

"You can have this room. Oh! The bed isn't made. I'll get some sheets." Charlie darted out of the room, and Sean was left alone.

The room was not overly large, but it was more than sufficient. The bed was small, but it definitely outsized the cot in his jail cell, and for that he was thankful. Sean moved to the window. He pulled the curtains back and one of them tore. He knew a moment of panic and then noticed that they were very faded, almost transparent.

"These are clean."

"The curtain tore. I'm sorry." Sean's voice was humble.

Charlie's eyes darted to the window. It was on the tip of her tongue to ask if he was usually so rough with things, but then she remembered how old the curtains were. They had been hanging there since her grandfather was alive.

"It doesn't matter. Here." She threw the sheets onto the bed. "Supper's in half an hour." On those words she exited, closing the door behind her.

twelve

Sean continued to stand next to the window, the events of the day going once again through his mind until a hunger pain tore at his stomach. The pain was impetus enough to cause him to move. Not wanting to dwell on the hours he had just lived through, he decided to make the bed.

He found himself mentally thanking his brother-in-law, Rigg, for the months he had lived with him. Rigg had taught him to take care of himself. Prior to that, his mother, and then his aunt, had seen to everything.

No water had been offered to Sean in jail beyond that which he'd been given to drink. So when the bed was finally made, and he noticed a pitcher and bowl on the dresser, he decided to find some water and have a quick wash. It couldn't really compare with a bath, but it would have to suffice and would certainly make him more presentable at supper.

Sean's door squeaked as it opened. Carrying the pitcher, he stepped tentatively into the hallway and walked softly out to the main room of the house where he stood looking around. There was no sign of his wife.

He noticed for the first time a large stove in the corner with wood stacked nearby. The kitchen table, appearing to be about four feet square, was made of oak and had four matching chairs.

Sean discovered that a doorway off the kitchen led to the living room. It had a long sofa and one overstuffed chair. There was a small table stacked with a few old newspapers, and all the furniture sat on an old, braided rug.

After a superficial inspection of both rooms, Sean looked more closely in the kitchen for a container of water. He had circled the room twice and figured he'd have to ask his wife or go without.

He turned to head down the hall and nearly dropped the pitcher he was carrying when he found Charlie standing just inside the room watching him.

"Is there a problem?"

"I was looking for some water." Sean gestured with the pitcher before noticing the shotgun in her hand and changing his mind about needing water. "I was going to have a quick wash, but it can wait."

His voice dropped on these last words; his whole body tensed. He wanted to move past her, but she was blocking his path and he wasn't about to do anything to make her use that gun. He stood still and waited.

"There's a well outside at the back of the house. I'll show you."

Sean watched in some surprise as she leaned her gun against a wall and preceded him to the door. Sean noticed as they walked that she was finally without her hat, and had even removed the oversized jacket she'd been wearing. There wasn't much to her; in fact, her frame was rather slight. She had the brightest red hair he'd ever seen.

There was no conversation as Sean filled his pitcher. Not until they were ready to go back to the house did Sean notice a bucket sitting beside the well.

"Charlotte," Sean used her name for the first time. "Do you want me to fill this for the house?"

Charlie's head had whipped around at the sound of her name, but there was no teasing in Sean's eyes. *No one* called her Charlotte, except in wisecracking, and Charlie just assumed that he was getting smart with her. She couldn't have been more wrong. His eyes were as respectful and hesitant as they had been since the two of them had stood in the courthouse and become man and wife.

"Yeah, we'll need it in the morning."

Sean proceeded to fill the bucket. Charlie stayed to watch him, although she wasn't sure why. For a moment in the kitchen she had thought he was out there to make a run for it, but that thought was swiftly put to rest when she had looked into his eyes.

Charlie was finally admitting to herself that his size had little to do with why she had married him. It had been his eyes. How many times were they going to get her into trouble? She had spoken up at the hanging because of those eyes and the way he'd kept them closed. Then in the kitchen, when she confronted him with the gun, it was the fear she saw in them that caused her to put the weapon down and escort him to the well.

Charlie had been amazed to see that he was afraid of her. She found she didn't care for that at all. She didn't plan to get close to this man in any way. They might be married, but in her mind he was nothing more than hired help. Yet to see a man of his size and obvious strength showing fear tugged at her heart.

❑ ❑ ❑

Sean set down the bucket in the kitchen and took the pitcher to his room. While they had been at the well, a young girl named Ruth had delivered a plateful of food from the hotel to Charlie's kitchen table. By the time Sean returned to eat, Charlie had carefully divided the food. He sat down in the chair across from her.

Sean, believing he could consume five times the amount on his plate, found himself suddenly queasy. He ate slowly of the beef stew before him, and when Charlie tried to pass him half of her biscuit, he declined. Though he found himself hoping there would be more food in the future, for now he was thankful that he had no more to tackle.

The meal was eaten in silence. By the time Charlie rose, Sean was also finished, and he watched as she put their plates in a large pan. She turned and spoke her last words of the evening.

"We start work at 6:00, so you'd better get some rest."

"I'll do that. Thank you for supper," Sean said softly. "Goodnight, Charlotte."

Charlie frowned again at the use of her name before watching him leave. The frown caused Sean to wonder what he had done this time.

❏ ❏ ❏

Sean's body was trembling with fatigue and something else he couldn't name by the time he crawled beneath the blanket on his bed. Even though the bed was too small, it felt wonderful to relax his tense muscles.

In a state of physical exhaustion, Sean thought he would fall right to sleep, but again the day's events began to play through his mind. One moment he was about to be hanged, and the next he was married. In quick succession the faces of Father, Rigg, Kaitlin, Marcail, Gretchen, and Molly all floated through his mind. Someday he might see them again. The thought was too much for him.

His hand came to the tender line on his neck where the rope had rubbed. This time he let the fear and helplessness come fully to mind. Tears flooded his eyes. He had cried in the jail cell right before the hanging, but these tears, in the house of a stranger who now happened to be his wife, made the earlier tears seem minor in comparison.

Sean's entire body shook with sobs, and he was unaware of the hoarse cries that issued from his throat. He thought he would never gain control, and in fact, didn't even try. He wept and thanked God he was alive, allowing himself for the first time to really believe it.

Unknown to Sean, Charlie stood in the middle of her bedroom and listened to his cries. Her face was a mask of shock and confusion. Before this time she would have said that the sound of a man's tears would disgust her, but not now, not this man's.

Charlie's heart was hard, but something was beginning to tear inside of her. She told herself that if he didn't stop soon, he was going to make her cry. And that was something she was sure couldn't happen, since she hadn't cried in years.

She listened until the tears stopped, and wondered what type of man her husband really was.

"My husband," Charlie said out loud, as if she had just realized this fact. She whispered, "What have I done?"

❏ ❏ ❏

Franklin Witt stood in the sheriff's living room, where he had tracked down Judge Harrison. The banker was fraught with frustration, since the judge would not listen to reason.

"Doesn't anyone recognize that we've let a bank robber loose? He has probably murdered Charlie and is
halfway to Hartley's hideout by now."

"I think you've got him all wrong, Witt. For one thing,
Charlie can usually take care of herself, and for another,
Sean is not violent. He's also not really loose, at least, not
the way you're talking about," Duncan assured him.
"I'll be keeping an eye on him, you can count on that."

Witt ran a distracted hand through his hair, and the
judge took pity on him.

"Go home now, Witt. The document was legal, and
there's nothing you can do. Maybe things will look better
in the morning."

Seeing that he had no choice, Franklin bid the men
goodnight. Once outside, he stood for a moment on the
porch and drew the night air into his lungs.

"Things might look better in the morning," he said to
himself as determination overtook him, "but I'm not
through with Sean Donovan. I'm sure he can tell me
more."

thirteen

Sean found himself wishing for a Bible as he dressed for the day. It had been a long time coming, but now with all his heart he'd love to read a few verses in God's Word. Some verses from Proverbs 3 came to mind, and Sean repeated these to himself as he dressed.

They were verses about trusting in the Lord for everything, instead of following your own heart. Even as Sean committed his future to doing just that, he couldn't help but wonder how different things might be if he'd done it five years ago. But no matter how he looked at the past, he was in Visalia now and married, and he'd best determine to follow God no matter what the future might bring.

He moved to the mirror and frowned at his reflection—he had no brush or comb. Before exiting his bedroom for breakfast, he finger-combed his hair and smoothed his beard, knowing it would have to do.

As he had expected, Charlie was already in the kitchen, and Sean approached slowly.

"Good morning."

"Morning," Charlie greeted him without turning from the stove. "You can sit down. I've got some pancakes near ready."

Sean did as he was told and thought the breakfast smelled wonderful. His mouth began to water.

Charlie came to the table a moment later bearing two plates. There were two large pancakes with a drop of applesauce on the side of each plate. The moment Charlie's body hit the chair she began to eat. She didn't rush, but she didn't take time for social amenities such as conversation or giving thanks for the food either.

Sean thanked God silently and began to eat. Since there didn't appear to be any other food, he told himself to go slowly. But Charlie was a good cook, and the first bite was too much for him. Within the space of a few seconds, Sean's plate was clean.

The pancakes did nothing toward appeasing Sean's hunger; in fact, they had only whet his appetite. He was reaching for his coffee when his stomach growled so loudly that he thought it might have been heard on the street.

"Didn't they feed you in jail?" Charlie asked softly.

"Yes."

Sean was careful not to look at his wife as he answered. He could feel the heat in his cheeks and lifted his cup to his lips hoping she wouldn't notice. He had been entertaining thoughts of shaving his beard if the opportunity presented itself, but if he was going to blush every time his wife looked at him, he just might reconsider.

Sean didn't know that neither his beard nor his cup did anything to hide the heating of his face, and Charlie watched in fascination as he flushed. She could hardly believe what she was seeing.

Charlie simply did not know what to think of this man. He was certainly unlike any bank robber she'd ever envisioned. He removed his hat when he spoke to her or entered a room. And he had actually attempted to help her from the wagon. He also blushed like a schoolboy in a roomful of little girls.

"There's more applesauce over there if you want it."

Charlie didn't know why she offered it to him, except that it felt funny to still be eating when the plate across the table was empty and the man behind the plate still hungry.

"Thank you," Sean spoke softly and carried his plate to the stove. The jar was almost empty, but Sean scraped out what he could and returned to the table. He was almost seated when he noticed that Charlie's coffee cup was empty, as was his own.

He didn't see the way Charlie was staring at him as he filled both cups until he'd again taken his seat at the table.

"I'm sorry," he said, gently contrite. "I saw your cup was empty and assumed you would want more."

"How'd you get to be a bank robber? You sure don't act like one."

The question surprised Sean speechless, and then he realized that everything about him, except possibly his looks, belied the situation in which they had first met.

"It's a long story," Sean finally answered after a few awkward moments.

Charlie shrugged. "I don't suppose it's any of my business anyway. And speaking of business," she stood abruptly, "we've got to get to work. Are you ready?"

"Sure," Sean answered, trying to ignore the hollow feeling in his stomach.

Charlie picked up her gun and led the way to the livery. Once inside she threw both sets of double doors wide open. Sean stood and watched her, wondering again when he should mention his experience.

"You ever feed stock?" Charlie asked abruptly.

"Yes, I have," Sean answered with relief, honestly wanting to help. "I've worked in a livery before."

Charlie's stance changed. "With a smithy?"

Sean nodded, and Charlie wanted to laugh at her good luck. She had been certain she was going to have to show this man everything.

"Good," she said simply, looking pleased without smiling. "There are three horses that need shoes. Head on into the forge and get started. I'll do the feeding."

Sean stood for a moment inside the forge and let his eyes caress the familiar tools of the trade. A smithy's job was long, backbreaking labor, but he had genuinely enjoyed the work and remembered it fondly as his gaze took in the anvil, forge, large bellows, drill bits, stocks and dies, and various hammers.

In the two years he had worked for the livery in Santa Rosa, he'd worked almost every aspect of the job from horse shoeing to wagon and halter repair. But never had the full weight of the job fallen on him before. Strangely enough, or perhaps not so strangely, he saw it as a challenge.

Hours later, Sean's shirt was soaked beneath his leather apron and the sound of pounding metal could be heard through the building. Charlie had been in to check on him from time to time, but satisfied with what she saw, she said nothing.

It was nearing 1:00 when Sean felt he needed food to finish the day. He went in search of his wife. He found her talking to a customer, and stood back as she finished.

The breeze was heavenly on his heated skin, and Sean had leaned back against the building and let his eyes slide shut. Charlie stabled a beautiful mare, and then joined Sean by the rear doors. It took him a moment to realize that she had drawn near and stood watching him.

In a move as automatic as breathing, Sean straightened and removed his cap. "I know there is a lot of work to be done, Charlotte, but if I'm going to finish the day I need something more to eat." Sean watched her brow lower, not understanding it was self-directed.

"You don't have to fix it," he quickly assured her, thinking she was angry. "I can get my own."

Charlie's last two smithies had never done anything but complain. When they weren't whining about something, they were talking with the customers and not getting any work done. Sean had achieved more in one morning than her last man could do in a week. He was obviously a hard worker and Charlie felt badly about not stopping him at lunchtime.

"The hotel delivers lunch and supper. I've told them to make it two plates from now on. Go on to the house and eat." None of this was spoken gently because Charlie was attempting to hide her dismay, but Sean didn't try to understand. He only nodded gratefully and walked away. Maybe he'd been wrong to ask about food, but his limbs were trembling so violently that all he cared about was making the front door and staying on his feet.

fourteen

That'll be the regular price, Murphy."

"Put it on my bill."

"You don't have a bill, and last time you left without paying. Now I'll have my money this time, or I'll keep your horse."

"Is that right?" came the belligerent reply. "Well, I'm leaving darlin' and you're welcome to try and stop me."

Not about to let this man walk out for the second time without paying, Charlie jumped forward and tried to grab the horse's bridle. Murphy shoved her away with ease. Sean, having finished his lunch, came through the back door just as she righted herself.

He watched in surprise as his wife moved forward to kick the tall man in the leg. Unfortunately, Sean was too far away to stop what happened next. Murphy turned back, and with one backward sweep of his hand, sent Charlie to the floor.

Murphy never heard Sean move, but he suddenly found himself spun around in time to see a fist flying with full force into his face. Sean didn't watch to see if Murphy got up before he went to his wife.

Charlie awoke to the feeling of straw at her back and the sight of a blurry man bending over her. Even before her eyes focused, the beard and hat told her it was Sean. She had no idea why he was bending over her and blinked to try to clear her vision.

"Charlotte?" Sean's voice was soft.

"Yeah," she answered as she lifted a hand toward her face, but Sean beat her to it. With tender care his fingers probed her jaw before gently sliding over her cheek. The left side of her face felt as though it was on fire.

They were both aware of voices and shouting on the street, but Sean didn't move away until Charlie was sitting up in the stall where he had laid her, and only then when he heard the sound of Duncan's voice.

"What's the problem?"

"I'll tell you what the problem is," a man Sean had never seen before said as he entered the livery. "I was walking by when our bank robber here decided to punch ol' Murphy in the face. I say he should've hung."

Murphy came to his feet, and started in with a string of curses and accusations that surprised no one. Duncan looked with regret at Sean, whose large frame blocked his view of Charlie. The sheriff was certain he had been right about this man, and even though Murphy was a trial to everyone in town, Duncan wasn't about to put one of Visalia's residents in danger. Having grown to like Sean made his job all the harder.

"It looks like I'll have to take you back to the jail, Sean, but I would like to hear your story."

Sean was livid with the loudmouthed man named Murphy, but for the moment his anger was directed at Duncan. "If the conditions on that paper state that I have to stand back while some man hits my wife, then you can go ahead and hang me!"

Duncan spun so fast on the foul-mouthed livery patron that Murphy took a hasty step backward into a pile of horse manure. "What is this, Murphy?" Duncan ground out the question, but he didn't wait for an answer.

"Charlie," he called, having just realized she was behind Sean. The young man stood his ground as the sheriff approached, his manner telling Duncan he had been right all along.

Duncan's hand briefly touched Sean's shoulder as he stepped around him and bent over the small livery owner. They spoke softly for some minutes while Charlie explained. Duncan saw red over the bruise on her face; her cheek was already beginning to swell.

Sheriff Duncan turned from Charlie to see that his deputy had come on the scene. In a quiet voice he ordered the deputy to take Murphy to the jailhouse and to keep him there until he arrived.

"He owes me money," Charlie called as Murphy started away.

"He can pay it too," a voice shouted out of the crowd. "He just cleaned me out in a game of poker."

There was laughter all around, and even though Charlie's head felt like it was going to fall off, she looked on with satisfaction as Murphy fished the coins from his pocket.

"Break it up now," Duncan shouted to the crowd that had gathered. Sean and Charlie stood quietly until the townspeople dispersed.

"You should put a cold cloth on that." Sean spoke quietly, watching his wife with very real concern and wishing he had a handkerchief or something to offer her.

"I'll be all right," she said, wanting to say more but afraid he would see the fierce emotions pouring through her. Besides, her face hurt too much to talk.

"I'll get back to work," Sean said.

"And I'll walk you to your house," Duncan told Charlie as he took her arm and headed for the rear door.

❑ ❑ ❑

"Get your feathers down, Charlie. I'm not offering you charity."

"I've got money."

"I know you do, probably more than most of us realize, but that man who has come to be your husband arrived with only the clothes on his back. If you don't need my money, then take some of your own and buy him an extra set of clothes and a haircut if he's so inclined. Honestly, Charlie, he can't even take those clothes off to wash them without having to go naked!"

Charlie nodded, realizing Duncan was right. The job of smith was very hard on clothing, and Charlie again felt badly at not noticing Sean's lack.

"How's the face?"

"What?" Charlie had completely forgotten that Duncan was sitting there, so intent was she on Sean's clothing.

"Are you sure you're all right?"

The tiny redhead shook her head. "I'm fine, Duncan," Charlie told him with a sigh.

"I think you should press charges."

"Oh, Duncan!" Charlie was now exasperated. "The way you carry on you'd think I'd never been hit before."

Now it was Duncan's turn to frown. He knew she spoke the truth, but it was her resignation to the fact that bothered him. A few minutes later Duncan excused himself, but his mind was still centered on Charlie Donovan, and he prayed with all his heart that Sean would make a difference in her life.

❑ ❑ ❑

Sean had to force back the groan he felt rising in his throat as he made his body sit down to supper. Every muscle in his arms and back was screaming. He couldn't remember the last time he had put in such a long, hard day.

Sean ate his chicken and corn, unaware of the way his wife watched him. She thought he looked ready to fall asleep in his plate. He was also filthy.

"If the conditions on that paper state that I have to stand back while some man hits my wife, then you can go ahead and hang me." Charlie believed that if she lived to be a hundred, she would never forget those words, uttered so protectively. They made her want to do something for him in return.

"My aunt runs the boardinghouse at the end of the block."

Sean looked up from his plate, wondering how he should reply to this, but Charlie went on.

"I don't have a tub, and she fixes me a bath anytime I want one." Sean continued to stare at her, and Charlie frowned a bit. "If you want, we can head over so you can have a bath tonight."

Sean wanted to weep with relief. He could barely tolerate his own stench. Instead he replied simply, "I would appreciate that."

Nothing more was said on the matter. When they were both finished with supper, Charlie led the way to a boxy, three-story house and without knocking, let them in the rear door.

fifteen

Is that you, Charlie?" The voice came from some-where in the bowels of the large house. Sean stood still while Charlie moved through the kitchen and beyond.

"It's me, Sadie," Charlie spoke as she found her aunt, down the hall and around the corner, in her tiny sewing room. She had a quilt on her lap and was stitching meticulously, near the window where the remaining sunlight poured through in an orange-red glow.

"Hi, honey," Sadie greeted her warmly.

"I came by for a bath."

Sadie immediately laid aside her sewing. "All right, I'll get it for you right now."

"It's not really for me."

Sadie's brows rose. Sitting back down, she eyed her niece speculatively. "I'd almost forgotten that congrat-ulations are in order."

Charlie didn't look at her aunt. Her gaze was focused on the quilt as though it was the most beautiful piece of work she had ever seen.

"What were you doing at that hanging, girl?" Sadie spoke softly.

Charlie shrugged. "I had to pick up supplies so I was in the area, and I'd heard he was young, and I just—"

"Where is he now?"

"In the kitchen."

Sadie looked stern for a moment and then rose with resignation. "Come on then, introduce me to your husband and I'll get his—" Sadie stopped suddenly as the light fell at just the right angle on Charlie's bruised face.

"That skunk oughta be shot," the older woman spat with fury and disgust. "Where was your *husband* when Murphy was plowing his fist into your face?"

"He came in right after." Charlie tried to defend him, but Sadie only shook her head and led the way to the kitchen. She didn't ask how Sadie knew about the incident; Sadie seemed to know most everything.

❑ ❑ ❑

Sean stood at the rear door, hat in hand, just where Charlie had left him. The kitchen was spacious, and the odors from supper lingered in the air; he guessed it might have been roast beef and potatoes.

The feeling of unreality was stealing back over him. Twenty-four hours ago he was about to be hanged. Suddenly he was married, working all day as a smithy, and now waiting for a bath in the home of his wife's aunt.

His wife. When was it going to sink in? Sean's mind went to the mixture of hostile and curious stares at the doors of the livery after he had flattened Murphy. His hand clenched in remembrance, and he knew he would do it again in a moment. No one was going to hurt Charlotte if he was around, and considering the terms of the document that Judge Harrison had explained before he'd married them, Sean was going to be around for at least the next five years.

Sean heard the voices of the women before they entered the room. He stood still, waiting for what he was sure would be a scene. He could just imagine what his wife's family must think of her marriage to a condemned man.

Sean watched as a woman of medium height and narrow frame walked into the room. Her hair was dark, with just a touch of gray, and was pulled into a fat bun on the top of her head.

"You can introduce me now, Charlie," Sadie instructed after she'd lit a lantern and inspected Sean from the top of his shaggy head to the tips of his grimy boots.

Charlie cleared her throat uncomfortably. "Sadie, this is my husband, Patrick Dono—"

"Sean," Sean interrupted softly, never taking his eyes from his wife's face. "I go by my middle name, Sean."

Charlie returned his look for the space of a second, and then introduced him as Sean Donovan. Upon the correct introduction, Sean's gaze swung to Sadie, whose face seemed to have softened from when she had first entered the room.

"Charlie tells me you want a bath."

"Only if it's no trouble," Sean said, his voice still soft.

Sadie couldn't believe her ears. She looked at Charlie, only to see that she was not the least bit surprised by her husband's considerate attitude.

"You don't act like a bank robber," Sadie blurted unthinkingly.

Sean glanced at Charlie. "So I've been told."

"Well, enough small talk." All at once Sadie became very brisk. "The big tub is in the pantry. You can drag it out here and I'll fill it for you."

"Do you suppose I could get something of Uncle Harry's from upstairs?"

"Sure, look in that trunk at the end of my bed." Sadie's gaze traveled over Sean's back as he hefted the tub in his arms. "There won't be anything to fit him, but at least he'll be covered while his clothes get washed."

❑ ❑ ❑

Sean let his body sink as far down into the tub as the sides would allow. The water had been almost too hot to touch when he'd first lowered himself in, but now it was just right, and Sean wished he could lay there all night.

He'd lathered up already and now his head rested on the rim of the tub. His knees were in the air. He let his eyes slide shut. It was then he heard the voices.

"I can't do that."

"Sure you can," came Sadie's kind voice. "I know things aren't like that between you, but he *is* your husband. Now just take these clothes to him and get his dirty ones."

"Can't you do it?"

Sean didn't hear the reply, but it must have been negative, for a few seconds later his wife entered the room. Sean had to force himself not to cover up, since he believed it would only make an embarrassing situation worse. Charlie, he noticed, was careful not to look anywhere but the floor, even when she addressed him.

"Here's a shirt and some pants that belonged to Sadie's late husband. I'll wash your other stuff when we get home."

"Thank you."

The soft, deep voice was enough to finally raise Charlie's eyes to her husband's, and she stared for a moment in fascination at the blush that covered his cheeks.

"When you're done, we'll go." The words were nearly stuttered in her haste, and Charlie exited the room just as swiftly.

Sean immediately reached for the length of toweling that Sadie had left, and then forced himself into the pants Charlie had brought him.

He emptied the tub outside. The opening and closing of the back door must have signaled the two women, for just as soon as Sean had his shoes on, Sadie and Charlie returned.

They both came to a complete stop just inside the kitchen door and stared at Sean. The borrowed pants were too tight and stopped two inches above his ankles. He hadn't buttoned the front of the shirt because the fabric wouldn't meet over his chest. The seams on the arms and shoulders were stretched to capacity. The women could only stare.

"Thank you for the bath," Sean finally said, breaking the uncomfortable silence. "And for the loan of the clothes."

Again Sadie looked at her niece. Her eyes seemed to be asking if this man was real or merely imagined.

Sean was relieved when Charlie moved toward the door. "Goodnight, Sadie, and thanks."

Sean nodded to the older woman and followed his wife. As soon as they reached the house, Charlie set to work washing her husband's clothes. He stood for a moment in indecision and Charlie, who read the fatigue in his eyes, sent him to bed.

"It'll be a while before you're accustomed to the work, so you'd better get all the rest you can."

"Thank you, Charlotte, and goodnight."

Charlie didn't reply, but she did move away from the wash basin to watch him as he moved down the hall and closed his bedroom door behind him.

sixteen

Sean wrapped a sheet around his waist the next morning and went in search of his clothes. The kitchen was empty, and there was no sign of his few belongings.

He had just headed back down the hall and knocked on Charlie's bedroom door when he heard her come in from outside. He retraced his steps to the kitchen and saw that she held his clothes in her arms.

"They dried on the line overnight," Charlie explained as she handed the clothes to Sean and tried not to look at his bare chest. It wasn't that she hadn't seen well-built men without their shirts; after all a livery had to have a blacksmith, but Sean was different.

Breakfast was plentiful on this morning, and Sean ate his fill. Charlie was cleaning up the plates when she spoke to Sean without turning toward him.

"We need to head to the general store first thing this morning so you can buy some clothes."

Sean hated to admit it, but wasted no time in doing so. "I have no money."

"I understand that," the redhead continued to talk with her back to him. "When Duncan was here yesterday he pointed out to me that I need to buy you a few things."

Sean said nothing; he couldn't get the words past the lump that suddenly rose in his throat. Duncan was the only person who felt real to him, and knowing that he was still thinking of him and cared enough to see to his needs was almost more than Sean could take.

Twenty minutes later they walked up the street together. The signs of a town coming to life were all around them. Doors were being opened and awnings raised. Sean had no idea where the store was; he simply followed his wife's lead. She suddenly stopped in front of the barbershop.

"Would you like a haircut?"

Sean's hand moved self-consciously to the shaggy hair at the back of his head. Before he could answer, Charlie held out a few coins to him.

"I'll go ahead to the store and find you some clothes. It's just three doors down. If you finish first, come down and find me."

For some reason Sean was hesitant to let her go, but she turned and moved confidently down the street, so he entered the near-empty shop.

There was a man in the chair who had been talking calmly until Sean stepped across the threshold. His face registered shock and then fear as soon as Sean took a chair against the wall.

Sean tried to ignore the man's stare, but his shame was so great that he didn't know where to look or if he should say something. It was a relief a few minutes later when the man left.

Sean stood when the barber swiveled the chair in his direction. For the first time he noticed the man showed none of the apprehension that his customer had displayed.

"Shave and a haircut?" He inquired solicitously.

Sean glanced at the coins in his hands. "Just a haircut, thanks."

As the sheet was draped around him Sean raised his chin. The chair was swiveled to face the mirror, and the barber began to snip.

"I think you got a lousy deal." The softly spoken words were such a surprise to Sean that he didn't immediately answer. The barber met his eyes in the mirror with such understanding that Sean relaxed.

"I had no business being in the bank in the middle of the night. It's a miracle I'm alive."

The barber smiled. "You're just like Duncan said you were. Did you want a shave and can't afford it, or do you prefer the beard?"

"I'm usually clean-shaven."

"Well then, since my sister, who happens to be married to Duncan, thinks you've got wonderful potential, the shave will be on the house."

"Your sister?"

"I believe she brought you a couple of meals while you were still in jail."

Sean remembered her then. She reminded him of his Aunt Maureen in San Francisco. She'd brought breakfast the morning after he had been arrested. Sean now saw the family resemblance in his barber. They were both round with graying hair and had full faces that brimmed with good health.

Sean's face was covered with lather before he could even say thank you, and within the space of about five minutes he was staring at a face he hadn't seen in months. He looked 17 again. What would Charlotte say?

He'd know soon enough since the barber was brushing him off and seeing him to the door. Sean stepped out onto the boardwalk. Replacing his cap, which fit differently without all the hair, Sean headed in the direction of the general store.

□ □ □

Charlie held a shirt up in front of her and wondered again if it was the right size. She had taken special note of how big his clothes were when she'd washed them, but now she felt uncertain. Preoccupied, it took a moment for her to realize someone had come up to stand behind her.

Sean watched her glance his way and then turn back to the shirt in her hands. An instant later her head whipped back around, eyes locked on his face. He watched as she took a hasty step backward, and quickly reached to steady her as she would have fallen into a low barrel of peanuts. He noted absently that his fingers met around her upper arm.

"Are you all right?"

"Yes." Charlie hated how breathless she sounded. "You just surprised me."

"I'm sorry."

"It's all right; in fact, I'm glad you're here. You need to tell me which of these will fit."

"There's no need to guess. Try it on," a man's voice called from behind the counter. "I wouldn't be able to resell it if people knew you'd taken it and brought it back."

The implication was not lost on either of them. Charlie's temper immediately flared, but Sean simply scooped up several shirts and headed into a small curtained room.

"How dare you talk to him like that, Pete!"

"It's the truth, Charlie, and you know it. He's a criminal and people are going to be wary."

"Well, he's never stolen a thing from your store, so there's no call to act like that. And another thing, he's my husband. I give a lot of business to this store, and if you're not going to treat Sean fairly, I'll start going across the street!"

Pete held his hands up in genuine contrition. "I'm sorry, Charlie. I'm just thinking of my need to make a living, and you know how it is in this town. Guilty or not, in the eyes of the people he's no good."

Because he was right, Charlie softened. "I'm sorry I snapped at you. Today we're in here to shop with honest coins and just want to be treated fairly."

"Fair enough," Pete nodded in agreement and, although still somewhat agitated, showed Charlie one of his new catalogs.

□ □ □

Sean had not missed one word of the conversation that had transpired in the next room. How did his wife expect people to react to his walking around town a free man, when most of them believed he should be six feet under ground? He felt sorry for her, since she obviously had more on her hands than she had bargained for. The thought troubled him.

But then without her, Sean would be dead. The sobering thought was enough to bring the young man back to the task at hand. He stepped back out into the store and waited for Charlie and Pete to notice him.

"Does it fit?" Pete asked, since Charlie seemed capable of little more than staring at Sean with his new haircut.

"I think the next size up, if you have it."

"Sure enough."

Sean disappeared back behind the curtain. Charlie wandered around the store then, and with Pete's help, picked up various items that she thought Sean might need. A special pleasure rose within her at his surprised look of gratitude when he watched Pete wrap their purchases.

Fifteen minutes later husband and wife were once again back on the street. Tucked safely under Sean's arm, in a wrapped parcel, were two pair of pants and three shirts, underclothes, socks, a comb and brush set, a razor, shaving mug and brush, and five handkerchiefs.

They received their fair share of curious stares, but no one appeared to be malicious. Even so, Sean was relieved to see the livery come into view. Charlie threw open the doors, and Sean headed toward the forge. The small ovenlike room was already comfortably familiar to him. Here there were no hostile or speculative looks.

The morning slipped away in quiet work. Sean found Charlie more than able as an assistant farrier. She seemed to know what a horse was thinking and second guessed movements on more than one occasion. Some horses tended to rest their weight on the man shoeing them. To call this a heavy burden was a gross understatement. Charlie had a little trick of pushing her small fist into the horse's flank. Most of the animals got the message, and Sean was able to go on with his work without gasping for air. They were just finishing with a high-spirited two-year-old when a young girl appeared with a tray.

"That's our lunch," Charlie said by way of explanation, and after securing the horse, led the girl to a crate.

"You can put it here, Lucy. Tell your mom I'll be in to pay my bill tomorrow."

The young girl, with a few covert glances at Visalia's resident outlaw, exited as silently as she had arrived. Charlie washed and set out their food while Sean had a quick wash himself. The crates were in the stall closest to the rear doors. The high separation wall of the stall shielded them from the people passing on the street, but still allowed the breeze from the back doors to reach them.

Sean looked eagerly at the food before him. Charlie must have been watching since she spoke up immediately.

"I've told the hotel to double your order for both lunch and supper. It might be more than you want, but then it'll be here in midafternoon if you're hungry."

"Thank you, Charlotte." Sean reached for his napkin. "It looks great."

And indeed it did. Large slices of ham nearly obscured one plate and the mix of carrots and potatoes was making Sean's mouth water. A jug of water, although not cold, was more than refreshing.

Sean, after laying his napkin on his knee, simply bowed his head and silently thanked God for the food. He had already reached for his fork and knife before he looked over to see Charlie watching him, her own fork halfway to her mouth.

"What were you doing just then?"

"Praying. Thanking God for the meal."

Sean couldn't hold back a smile as Charlie's head tipped back and she examined the rafters of the livery.

"Do you think Someone really heard you?" Her voice was sincere.

"Yes I do," Sean answered with surety, and Charlie went on to eat her food. Her face, still framed by her hat, gave nothing away.

seventeen

Franklin Witt did not have a personal grudge against Sean Donovan. In the hours following the hanging, however, he could think of little else except that he felt cheated. At first he was angry that Donovan hadn't swung from a rope, and then he got to wondering if maybe Sean could be of more use alive. The thought nagged him until he decided to see Duncan with an idea.

"What can I do for you, Witt?" Duncan asked as the suave banker entered his office first thing one morning.

"I've been thinking some more about Donovan." Witt forestalled Duncan with a raised hand when it looked like he was going to interrupt.

"I know you think I'm wasting my time, but the truth is, it's my time and he's still the best lead we've got. I'd just like to talk to him once more."

Duncan looked doubtful, and Witt hurried on.

"No strong-arm stuff, Duncan. I just want to appeal to him as one citizen of Visalia helping another."

Duncan could see how distasteful that last sentence was for Witt and in all honesty he couldn't say as he blamed him. The men talked about the bank robberies a moment more, and then Duncan assured Witt that he'd at least think on the idea.

"You have heard what a good worker he is, haven't you?"

"Yes, Duncan, I'll give him that. He does seem to be faring far better than I ever imagined, but I've got one more thing I need to say before I go. If that bank is hit again in the very near future, it won't matter if *you're* his alibi, you know there will be a lynch mob. Think on that, would you, Duncan?"

Duncan sat very still as Witt rose and left the office. He was right; there was no doubt in that. But right didn't make it fair. Of course, no one ever promised this life would be fair. It looked like Duncan would have to talk with Sean about the robberies whether he wanted to or not.

❑ ❑ ❑

Sean and Charlie settled into a pattern of sorts that saw them through the rest of the week. Lunch was always eaten in the livery, on the crates that served as a makeshift table and chairs. In the evenings they ate at the small kitchen table and then moved into the tiny living room where Charlie would usually repair a bridle as Sean read silently.

As soon as Charlie found out that Sean liked to read, she had the newspaper sent over. He was quickly seeing how trusted she was in town. Food, laundry, and even the newspaper were delivered without question.

By Saturday Sean was feeling a very definite change taking place in his body. The hours spent with a hammer in his hand pounding iron and pulling the bellows once again became easy.

Both Sean and Charlie went to Sadie's for baths Saturday evening after supper. On the way home Charlie told Sean the livery was closed on Sundays.

"Every Sunday?" Sean was visibly pleased.

"Yes. It used to be open every day all year, but business is always slow on Sunday, and the hotel has a small stable at the rear of the building for folks coming in on weekends. So all I do now is feed and water morning and evening. The doors are shut all day. Sometimes I take a buggy out if one of the horses hasn't had much exercise, but that's not really work."

Sean loved it when she talked to him. It didn't happen often, but when she did open up she usually had a lot to say. And then, he'd watch as an unsure look would pass over her face as though she had said too much, revealed too much of who she was.

"Oh!" Charlie's voice told him she had just thought of something. "I always eat Sunday dinner at Sadie's, so we'll be going there around noon."

"Are you sure that invitation is extended to me?" Regret rose deep from within Sean and shone in his dark brown eyes.

They had arrived back at the house now and Charlie stood in the kitchen looking with great compassion at him. "Sadie likes you. I can't say that all the people in the boardinghouse are going to welcome your presence, but what Sadie says, goes. She told me tonight when we left that she would see us *both* tomorrow."

Sean was pleased by the invitation, but more than a little wary. He had no desire to cause trouble for Charlie's aunt. His presence at the boardinghouse dinner table would be like inviting it in through the front door.

Sean and Charlie had no more time to discuss Sunday dinner because someone was knocking on the door. It was Duncan.

"I'm sorry to disturb you on a Saturday night, but I need to talk with Sean."

Charlie held the door wide and Duncan removed his hat and stepped into the room. Charlie gestured both men into the living room and followed, taking one end of the sofa. Sean sat next to his wife, and then looked to Duncan who had taken the chair.

"Franklin Witt was in to see me this week," Duncan began without preamble. "He'd like to talk with you, Sean. He's holding out a faint hope that there's something you overlooked that might lead us to Hartley."

"I told you all I know, Duncan."

"I'm sure you did. Witt would like to talk with you anyway. I think it might be a good idea, if for no other reason than to give him some peace of mind."

Sean looked at Charlie, who had tensed when Duncan mentioned Witt and then Hartley. Husband and wife stared at one another for a moment, and Sean would have given much to know what she was thinking.

Duncan didn't stay long, but before leaving he arranged for Sean to come to his office on Monday at 8:00. "By the way, Sean, bring Charlie with you on Monday. There's no reason for her to stay away."

"All right, Duncan. Goodnight."

Sean shut the door and turned to find Charlie on the threshold between the kitchen and living room. Again Sean watched her, wishing he knew her thoughts, or at least what to say.

"I'm pretty tired. I think I'll go to bed."

"Are you all right?" Sean could not hold the question back.

"I don't know," Charlie answered, wondering herself. "Witt just isn't one of my favorite people, and I don't want to see you used by him."

Not knowing how to answer, Sean changed the subject. "If you want I can get up and do the chores in the morning. You could sleep in."

"Thanks, but I'm an early riser. Goodnight, Sean."
"Goodnight."

❏ ❏ ❏

Three hours later Charlie was convinced that this was anything *but* a good night. She'd tossed and turned for what seemed like days. Never had she known such a myriad of emotions over anything in her life, and certainly never a man.

She had stood and watched Sean pound iron into horseshoes and then those same hands, as gentle as those of a nurse, slid tenderly along her bruised jaw.

And again, when she had nearly fallen in the general store, he had grasped her arm ever so lightly, but with enough strength to let her know she wouldn't fall.

It had taken until the next day for Charlie to find out that Sean had only thrown one punch before Murphy hit the floor. And then those same hands, lightly clutching his napkin, had paused to pray before eating.

Prayer. Sean was the only adult Charlie knew who actually prayed. She thought such petitions were for children before they figured out that no one was there listening. Charlie had prayed until she was 12. She had asked God every night to give her a pony of her own and to make her grandfather stop hitting her. But there was no one up there, so naturally her prayers went unanswered.

Sean however, believed in Someone. Charlie could see that. He didn't seem to be the type of man who prayed without belief. But what type of man *was* he? The question plagued Charlie until she fell into a fitful sleep. In the morning she wished she'd taken Sean up on his offer to do the chores.

eighteen

Sean wore the still-new pants and shirt on Sunday morning. The shirt was a blue-and-white check, and the pants were a heavy denim. Freshly shaved and with his hair brushed into place, Sean cut a handsome figure.

The moment he opened his bedroom door, he could hear Charlie moving around the kitchen preparing breakfast. He wondered if his wife was thankful that even though she could cook, she had the means to have lunch and supper delivered after she'd worked all day.

Sean's thoughts moved to May Taylor, his sister Kaitlin's mother-in-law. She was a woman who for years worked all day in Santa Rosa's shipping office and then went home to prepare supper for her family. Of course her sons were helpful, but it had to take some of the edge off one's appetite to be so tired when eating.

"Good morning," Sean greeted Charlie as he stepped into the room.

"Morning," she answered, and Sean thought she sounded like she was getting a cold.

"How are you this morning?"

"Fine."

Sean doubted that, but was hesitant to press her. He thought of another tack.

"Why don't you let me finish breakfast?" Charlie stopped, a cracked egg poised over her bowl, and stared at him. Sean continued, "You've already done the chores, and I haven't done a thing today, so—"

"You can cook?"

"Sure. My brother-in-law taught me."

Charlie turned fully away from the bowl now. "You have family?"

"Yes, I do," Sean spoke as he stepped forward and rescued the dripping egg from her hand. "A father, two sisters, a brother-in-law and two nieces, last I knew."

"Do they know about—" Charlie hesitated.

"About the hanging?"

Charlie nodded.

"No. I haven't seen any of them for two years," Sean said as he stared intently at the eggs in the bowl.

"Where do they live?"

Glad for any question to distract his painful thoughts, Sean answered promptly. "Everyone is in Santa Rosa except my father—he lives in Hawaii. If you haven't heard of it, it's a group of islands out in the Pacific Ocean."

Charlie watched as he held the bowl in his arm and beat the eggs furiously with a fork. Once again she was overcome with curiosity about this man.

"Why is your father in Hawaii?"

"He's a missionary."

Charlie blinked in surprise, and then her face lit with understanding. "That's why you pray before meals," she almost whispered, "because your father is a missionary."

Sean knew he had to weigh his next words carefully. "With missionary parents, I probably did learn about prayer at a younger age than some, but that's not why I pray now."

It was on the tip of Charlie's tongue to say "why do you?" but she suddenly thought she might be intruding. Instead she picked up on something else he had said.

"You didn't mention your mother."

"She died when I was 14." Even now it pained Sean to say those words. "We were at my aunt's house in San Francisco. None of us knew she had tuberculosis until the end. We had a few good weeks together, and then she died quietly one afternoon during her nap."

This time it was Sean's turn to wonder if he had shared too much. Talking about his mother made him feel vulnerable, and once again he concentrated on breakfast.

Some five minutes later they sat down together to a meal of scrambled eggs with bits of salt pork. Sean had also fried large slices of bread. Charlie's contribution was her great-tasting coffee.

There was no conversation about who would wash or dry, but both husband and wife pitched in after the meal to clean the kitchen.

Sean moved into the living room to read the newspaper and was pleased to see Charlie join him. By the time they had finished with the dishes, she'd grown quite pensive, and Sean was glad to see that she wasn't trying to avoid him. There had been something on his mind from the first night he'd come here, and he knew now was finally a good time to mention it.

"Charlotte," Sean called her name and waited for her to look up from her account books. "I've never thanked you for what you did for me at the hanging. It took a lot of courage to come forward and marry a bank robber. I'm not really sure why you did, but I do know I'm grateful and in one sense, I owe you my life. Thank you."

Charlie didn't know what to say. She certainly realized that he'd have hung if someone hadn't stepped forward, but she never expected to be thanked for it.

"You're welcome," she finally spoke softly, knowing by the way Sean watched her that he was waiting for a reason.

"I also want to thank you for all you've given me. You didn't owe me a thing, but you've dressed me and fed me like a king, and well, thanks for that too."

He completely flustered her this time. She sounded almost irritated when she spoke.

"Well, it's not as if you haven't worked for it. I mean, blacksmith work is hard, and well, that's why I married you."

It suddenly occurred to Sean as he watched and listened to his wife that she hid her true feelings behind a mask of irritation when she was upset. Sean was usually much better at hiding his feelings than she, even if he did blush every once in a while, and he felt real compassion for the upset he'd caused in her life.

"Would you like to go for a ride in the buggy?" The question seemed to come out of nowhere, and Sean saw that she was trying to make amends for what she had said.

"I think that's a great idea."

"Good," Charlie replied, looking so relieved that Sean smiled. "Sadie doesn't expect us for a good two hours, so we have plenty of time."

Not for a moment did Charlie consider asking Sean to pull the buggy out or hitch the horse. She had gone out ahead of him and was almost finished by the time he arrived. He stood by rather helplessly as she climbed aboard, and couldn't help but remember how often he'd seen Rigg lift Kaitlin into the wagon. Kaitlin had seemed to expect it, and he knew Rigg enjoyed doing this small service for his wife.

As usual, none of these feelings showed on his face, and Charlie simply looked at him expectantly as she sat on the seat, holding the reins loosely in her grip.

Sean climbed aboard and they headed out the back doors. The day was growing hot, but the top was in good shape. The canopy afforded them plenty of protection from the sun. Cooper's Livery also had a surrey, but there was no need for the extra seat, and it had no top.

Sean got to thinking about what fine equipment and horses the livery had, and said as much to Charlie.

"That's the way my grandfather liked things," she explained. "He believed that if you invested in your own business, people would trust you to do right by them, thus expanding and paying you back for your investment."

"He sounds like he had a good head for business. I take it your grandfather is no longer living."

"He died six years ago. I've been running things on my own ever since."

"And doing a good job, from what I've seen."

Charlie smiled at the compliment, and Sean leaned back in the seat to watch what he could see of her profile. He began to wonder why she was so seldom without her hat. And why, when she obviously had such a prosperous business, she didn't buy clothes that fit.

Her blouse was so full it seemed she might be able to fit another person inside, and her skirt, although the proper length, seemed to have an unusual number of gathers at the waist. The more he thought about it, the more sense it made. After all, she had a very physical job, and to be confined by tight clothing could hinder her work.

Charlie talked as the buggy moved through town. She told Sean about the different people in the area, and once in a while asked Sean questions, but the conversation never ventured to the personal. It was a very relaxed time, and Sean was a little surprised when he suddenly realized Charlie was pulling up in front of Sadie's.

His feeling of contentment evaporated. At that moment, Sean was certain he could relate to those long-ago Christians as they entered the arena filled with hungry lions.

nineteen

Tansy Lang was a flirt, and she made no apology about it. Since she worked in the hotel dining room, it was unusual that she would even be at Sadie's table for dinner on Sunday, but she was there, making Sean wish he wasn't. He had prayed so specifically, asking God to help him bear up under the hostile looks and words he was sure to find. But nothing could have prepared him for Tansy.

She seemed to find it exciting that he'd robbed a bank, and in her high-pitched voice told him so at least ten times. Her dress did a fine job of exposing her cleavage. But it didn't seem to be enough for Tansy, who was intent on drawing Sean's attention to her chest by leaning toward him every few moments. He finally trained his eyes across the table on his wife, who wouldn't look at him, and tried valiantly to get through the meal.

There were six other people at the table besides Sadie, Tansy, Charlie, and himself, but Tansy, who was seated next to him, had so monopolized the entire conversation that Sean had no idea how people felt about his presence.

After the meal, which Sean barely tasted, Sadie directed him and Charlie to a small sitting room back by the kitchen. He was thankful that no one else joined them as they sat down on the long sofa. An uncomfortable silence enveloped them.

"Charlotte," Sean spoke up because he couldn't let the question wait. "Does Tansy eat lunch here every Sunday?"

Charlie was so shocked by the question that she didn't immediately answer. Sean suddenly stood up, his agitation very clear.

"Because if she does," he went on, "I won't be back."

Charlie could do nothing more than stare at him. She had been so intent on her own misery that she never once considered how Sean might be feeling.

Tansy's clothing always showed off her full breasts and tiny waist, and for the first time Charlie had felt like an old crow in her presence. Tansy's nails were attractively long, and her hands were never rough like those of a livery owner's. The woman had stood back while Sean seated her, and then thanked him by leaning close and whispering something in his ear.

Charlie had not waited for anyone to seat her, and she felt her face burn as one of the older women at the table raised a wrinkled brow in her direction. From that point on, Charlie couldn't watch anything that went on across the table.

"Does she, Charlotte?"

The question brought Charlie back to earth. "No. She works at the hotel, and actually she's never here on Sundays. I think she's been under the weather and taking a few days off work."

Sean relaxed, and Charlie searched for something to say. She spotted her aunt's paper.

"You didn't get to finish the newspaper. Why don't you sit down and read Sadie's?"

Sean took up the offer and settled back down on the sofa. There was probably more they should have said to each other regarding Tansy's behavior, but Sean watched Charlie reach for a catalog on a nearby table, so he began to read the paper.

There was no conversation. The only noise was the gentle rattle of paper as Sean turned from page to page. He glanced over a few times to see that Charlie seemed to be stuck on one page in the catalog. It was a listing of blacksmith supplies.

"Can't decide which one you like?"

"No, I guess I can't. I hate it when they don't show pictures of all of them."

"Doesn't it describe the difference next to the prices?"

Charlie hesitated for only a second. "I think it probably does, but I can't read."

Thankful her gaze was on the catalog for a few seconds longer, Sean was given time to school his features.

"Want me to read it to you?"

"You don't mind?"

"Not at all." His voice was gentle.

Charlie scooted closer and handed the catalog to her husband. The front brim of her hat was flipped back and she looked up expectantly as Sean began to read. After starting to read he glanced down to see if she was listening, and for the first time noticed the beautiful color of her eyes—a deep hazel.

He read the whole page with an occasional question from Charlie, and then asked if she wanted him to go on.

"No, you read everything I need to know. I'll just look at the pictures for a while."

Sean returned the catalog and picked up the newspaper, but he couldn't concentrate. On every page of print he saw her eyes and the intent way she held her head as she listened to him read from the catalog. Sean glanced repeatedly out the corner of his eyes to look at her. He noticed at one point that she was falling asleep.

He shifted and pulled the small pillow from his far side and put it against his opposite hip.

"Charlotte," his voice was soft. "Lay your head here and rest a bit."

Charlie turned and blinked owlishly at him, but then did as he bade. Once her head was settled on the pillow, she picked her feet up off the floor and curled her legs on the seat.

Sean gently tugged her hat off and smoothed her hair as she fell into slumber. He sat looking down at her for a long time.

"Sleep well, Charlotte, because tomorrow I'm going to start teaching you to read."

The words were whispered, but Sadie, who had finally finished her dinnertime cleanup, heard every syllable. She didn't enter the room as planned, but turned and went to her sewing room where she pulled a hankie from her sleeve and wiped her suddenly wet eyes.

twenty

Cooper's Livery had opened before 7:00 every morning for as long as anyone could remember, but this was the second day since Charlie Cooper had become Charlie Donovan that the doors remained shut.

Sean and Charlie made a point of being on time to the sheriff's office, and they found both Duncan and Witt waiting.

Witt seemed to be good at his word and did not do anything to put Sean under pressure. Witt was silent as the four adults were seated, but then Sean remembered Charlie's comment about Witt using people, and decided to keep his guard up.

Duncan opened. "Thanks for coming in, Sean and Charlie. Though this discussion was not my idea, I'm not against it. I think I'll just stay quiet while Witt here asks his questions."

Witt's manner was very sedate as he began to question Sean. His voice seemed almost gentle to Sean, and then he realized the older man was in deep thought.

"Are you certain you don't know where Hartley's cabin is?"

"Very certain. I spent some time last night thinking

on the terrain, and I know we were in the hills to the east, but beyond that, I haven't a clue."

"Has Hartley contacted you?"

Sean look so surprised that Witt nearly told him to forget the question.

"No, not once. If he did though, I would come to Duncan immediately."

They talked for a while longer, and then Witt surprised Sean by standing and offering his hand. Sean stood also, and they shook hands. Witt thanked everyone in the room and left quietly.

"Well," Charlie breathed after the door shut, thinking maybe she had misjudged the man. He hadn't been at all the tyrant she'd expected, and she said as much to Duncan.

"I've been telling him that Sean is not the man he believes him to be. Maybe he's starting to see that for himself."

"I really wish I could have been more help," Sean admitted.

"You did fine. I know you need to get to the livery, but I need to talk with both of you." Duncan hesitated, praying as he had been for days, about what needed to be said.

"It's time, Sean, that you establish yourself as a law-abiding citizen in this town. Now I don't want to completely upset your life, Charlie, although you did that to some extent when you married Sean. What I'm trying to say is—get involved. Start attending a church, our social events, anything this town has to offer. The townspeople will be watching the way you treat each other. I've already heard about the tongue-lashing you gave Pete the other day. He was stunned that you defended Sean, but also fascinated since your relationship is a curiosity.

"Sean, you need to be in touch with your family and ask them to write you. It would go a long way toward the good for you to get mail. I'm sure most people think you have no previous home or family. They seem to think criminals crawl out from under rocks."

Duncan stopped talking and stared at the thunder-struck couple who both craved privacy in the new and uncomfortable marriage in which they found themselves.

"Why?" Charlie finally asked in a small voice.

"Because," Duncan said gently, "if Hartley hits the bank again, and Sean has stayed aloof and separated from the community, no one will believe he wasn't involved in some way. Your testimony would be of no value, Charlie, because the talk in town is that you're falling for your new husband."

Duncan watched her face heat up like a flame. He knew his words were blunt, but he didn't see any help for it at this point. "Talk it over and don't forget, if you need *anything*, I'm available day or night."

It was a quiet young couple who exited the sheriff's office and then stood outside on the boardwalk. Sean knew that any move they made would have to be initiated by Charlie. He wasn't going to ask or suggest anything. He had turned Charlie's life upside down, and even though the end result could be his being blamed for a crime he did not commit, he was not going to pressure her into an action she couldn't abide.

"He's right, you know."

Sean stared down at the woman next to him, not really believing she'd spoken. But then she continued.

"We do need to get involved, and I think you should pick up some writing supplies today so you can get in touch with your family."

Sean stepped off the walk to lessen the difference in their heights, but still had to dip his head to see his wife's face. She had spoken with her head down, and the rim on her hat completely hid her features from his view.

Not until Sean had dipped his head did Charlie look at him. Her look was such a mixture of fear and determination that he wanted to hold her.

"Are you sure?" he asked softly.

"I'm sure," she said, meeting his gaze for the space of a few heartbeats. When Charlie moved in the direction of the general store, Sean followed her.

❑ ❑ ❑

Sean had been standing next to Charlie for five minutes while she inspected the writing supplies. He wasn't sure why she was taking so long, but she seemed in no hurry. He put his hands behind his back, rocked back on his heels, and told himself to bide his time.

"I didn't realize how many different things you could buy." Sean heard her soft comment and finally understood. She was fascinated with the paper and ink. She had never even looked at it before. Sean watched her turn, tip her head back, and look up at him.

"Maybe you'd better pick something out. I never buy anything more than the cheapest paper and a pencil to do my accounts."

Sean leaned forward and spoke softly. "Anything you pick out will be fine."

Charlie looked up into his sable brown eyes. *Is this the way you feel about life when you've had such a close brush with death? You don't ask for much and expect even less?*

"Are you always so agreeable?"

Sean's brows rose on what he believed to be a cryptic question, and Charlie looked embarrassed.

"I don't think Murphy thinks I'm agreeable." A sparkle entered Sean's eyes. Charlie almost smiled. Sean realized in that instant how little he had seen her smile, and silently begged her to grin at him. But it was not to be. She turned back to the paper, quills, and ink and made a quick selection.

Just as they were walking away from the supplies Sean spotted an elementary school primer. "Get this too." Sean's voice brought Charlie back around, and after one glance at the book in his hand, her startled gaze shot to his face.

Sean remained expressionless as she frowned at him, and when she didn't immediately reach for the book his eyes once again lit with laughter and he spoke.

"Still think I'm agreeable?"

Charlie's eyes narrowed. He was teasing her! The thought so startled her she almost laughed. *But that wouldn't do at all*, she told herself, and snatched the book from his hand, throwing a comment over her shoulder about the horses shoeing themselves.

Sean stood for an instant watching her stalk away to the counter where Pete was waiting. After a brief moment of thought, he followed very slowly.

twenty-one

Dear Kaitlin,

I know you're going to be surprised to hear from me, and all I can do is humbly ask your forgiveness for the way I left and the length of time I've been out of touch.

So much has happened, it's hard to know where to begin. Aunt Maureen probably told you I'd been to see her, but I didn't stay long. The way I spent my time from that point to the present is not near so important as where I am today.

Almost two weeks ago I was sentenced to hang for a bank robbery I'd been a part of in Visalia. I was on the gallows, the rope around my neck, when a woman came forward and offered to marry me. (It's a law in this county that you can be pardoned under certain circumstances and by such an action.)

I was married immediately to Charlotte Cooper. She owns and runs the livery and needed me to smith for her. I am thankful to be alive and to finally see that God has been with me all along, but it's a tremendous burden on my heart to be married to an unbeliever. Please pray with me that Charlotte will come to know Christ.

There was no easy way to tell you this; I just hope it's not too direct. Please write me soon. If I could come to you, I would. But in many ways, my life is no longer my own.

There is so much more to share, but knowing that your worry has been long, I feel an urgency to get this mailed. How is Marcail? Please tell her I love her. Have you heard from Father? Apologize to Rigg for me and thank him for the brotherly love he's always shown. Please kiss the girls and give them my love.

Sean

Sitting at the kitchen table, Sean broke down at this point. He asked himself repeatedly how he could have left his loving family, and why he'd been so blind to how much they cared. What if something had happened to Katie or Marcail and he would never see them again?

The questions tormented him, causing his tears to come harder. He prayed and tried to give his hurt to God, but it was some minutes before he was able to contain himself. Even then his heart felt bruised over all he'd left behind.

Around the corner in the living room, Charlie was crying with him. She was beginning to care deeply for him and this made her pain nearly as great as his.

Charlie listened as Sean tried to gain control of himself. She wanted to join him in the kitchen but was sure she would be intruding. As it was, she didn't have long to wait before he joined her in the living room.

Sean entered the room and glanced at Charlie as she worked over her books. He sat on the sofa and picked up the paper. He'd read just a few sentences of one article when he felt her eyes on him. He looked over and forced his eyes to lock with hers.

"Are you all right?"

"I think so," he answered honestly. "Thank you for getting the supplies so I could write."

"You're welcome," Charlie answered and then hesitated. "Do you think they'll write back?"

"I'm sure they will."

"Then you didn't tell them about the bank robbery?"

Sean understood instantly. She was talking about conditional love, probably the only kind she had ever known. He chose his words carefully.

"I did tell them about the robbery and the hanging. They will be upset that I was almost hanged, but it's been so long since I've been in touch I think they'll be glad I'm alive and that I wrote to them."

"So you're not afraid they'll never want to see you again?"

"No, that thought never entered my mind."

Charlie was quiet for a long time, and Sean just stared at her. "Your family must be a very understanding one." Sean watched as she went back to her accounts, a sign that the conversation was over.

What type of family life had she known? The question moved through Sean's mind for some minutes before he went back to his paper. As he did, he spotted the school primer sitting on the living room table. His eyes swung once again to Charlie, and he wondered how she even handled her account books. Sean sighed mentally. He knew he couldn't possibly bring it up tonight, but at some point he had to offer to teach his wife to read.

twenty-two

At breakfast the following morning, Sean's attempt to bring up the school primer failed. Charlie became very brisk and said she wanted to open early since they had been late the day before. Sean headed to the post office to post his letter and then to the livery, praying for a chance to talk with her.

There were several opportunities during the day, but each time Charlie avoided Sean neatly. As the day wore on, Sean became more determined to discover if Charlie was upset with him or just did not want to learn to read. He decided to wait until evening, when she had no place to go, and ask her outright.

"Who does the cooking for the hotel?" Sean asked as they sat down to their evening meal

"Ruth's mom," Charlie replied.

"She's a great cook."

"Most of the town thinks so, and of course her husband does too."

"I haven't met him, have I?"

"You must not have, because you would remember. His size alone will tell you that he's his wife's biggest fan."

"I could fatten up on your cooking too," Sean commented. "Fortunately I work it all off during the day."

"Do you think the work is too hard?" Charlie was instantly concerned, and then embarrassed.

"No," Sean said, ignoring her heated cheeks. "The work is fine. You have some of the best equipment I've ever seen."

They ate in silence for a time and then Sean nonchalantly brought up the primer.

"Charlotte, I wanted to talk to you about the book I had you buy yesterday."

"I think I want to go see Sadie tonight."

Sean knew he shouldn't have been surprised by this, but he was. How long was she going to avoid him? It was a question that went unanswered because Sean decided once again to let the matter drop. Charlie was good at her word, and as soon as the dishes were done, they headed to Sadie's.

❏ ❏ ❏

"What's this for?" Sadie held out the coins that Charlie had just placed in her lap. Sean was having a piece of pie in the kitchen, and Charlie had gone in search of her aunt. She had found her in the small room Sadie called her private parlor.

"I'm not good with picking out fabrics."

"Fabric for what?"

Charlie frowned, not really wanting to tell, but not seeing that she had any choice.

"A dress."

"For you?"

Charlie nodded without looking at her aunt. Sadie's fingers went under her niece's chin so she would have to look at her.

"What's going on?"

Charlie shrugged and then softly explained what Duncan had said to them. "I think he's right, and I don't have a thing to wear to church."

"So you think you would actually care if Sean had to go back to the gallows?"

Charlie frowned at her aunt. "Of course I would; he's the only blacksmith I've got."

Sadie chuckled. "I guess he is at that. How silly of me to think you might be feeling something for him."

Tears filled Charlie's eyes, and Sadie was instantly contrite. "I'm sorry honey. I shouldn't tease you. I'll go first thing tomorrow and get the fabric. In fact, let me measure you right now, and I'll have a dress ready for you to try on tomorrow night."

"Really?"

"Really," Sadie said with a smile, thinking that Charlie looked young again for the first time in years.

"Sadie?"

"Yes?"

"Can we please not tell Sean?"

Sadie looked surprised, and then her eyes grew round with feigned ignorance. "Tell Sean what?"

Charlie gave her aunt a hug. Sadie went out to check on her niece's husband and give him another piece of pie. Then the two women slipped quietly into Sadie's sewing room so Charlie could be measured.

"There isn't much to you under all these baggy clothes, is there?"

Charlie looked down at her small figure under a nearly worn-out camisole. "You think I'll look all right in the dress?"

"I think you'll look like an angel. Just remember, a man treats a lady like a lady when she acts like one. How you look is not near so important as how you act."

Charlie was quiet as she took this in. Her mind conjured up the scene when Tansy allowed Sean to hold her
chair; not just allowed it, but expected it. Charlie's eyes
closed in pain as she remembered Sean staring at her
those times she had climbed aboard the wagon or buggy
like a man.

The more Charlie thought about it, the more she realized she had no idea how a lady acted. Did a man always
help a woman with her chair, and how about the wagon?
Her grandfather never once helped her or Sadie into or
out of a wagon. Of course, her grandfather had been no
gentleman, and Sean Donovan was.

Any man who would remove his hat when he entered
a room and stand when a woman walked into his presence was a gentleman from the toes up.

"I wonder what his mother was like?"

"Whose mother?"

"Sean's."

"Charlotte," Sean called from the other room before
Sadie could reply.

"I'll be out in a minute," Charlie responded, hoping
he wouldn't come to find her. She slipped her blouse
back on and hurried with the buttons.

Sean was standing near the table, his plate empty once
again. That he had wondered where she was and why he
had been deserted in the kitchen was obvious.

"Are you ready to go?" Charlie asked.

"Not if you're busy," Sean replied.

Always so considerate, Charlie thought, and then called
a farewell to her aunt.

The couple walked side by side toward home in the
gathering dusk. They were almost to the livery when a
voice, slurred with inebriation, came out of the gloom.

"Well, if it isn't the newlyweds."

"Get out of here, Murphy," Charlie told him in disgust.

Murphy ignored her and began to rain insults down on the livery, its owner, and Sean. At one point he waved his arm expansively and nearly fell over into the street. The action seemed to break his concentration. He stared at Charlie as though just noticing her, and then stumbled on into the night.

Charlie waited only the space of two heartbeats before she started after him. Sean's reactions were quicker, though. In one deceptively fast move his arm shot around her waist, and he pulled her back against his chest.

"Let go of me, Sean," she panted in fury as she struggled against his hold. "I'm going to give Murphy a kick he's never going to forget."

"I think it would be best for everyone if I just held onto you for a while." Sean's voice was so rational that Charlie wanted to scream. She continued to pull at his arms, both around her now, but it was like a dragonfly trying to move a horse's hoof off its wing.

"Weren't you listening to the things he said?" Charlie fumed, trying another tactic. "The things he said about *you*?"

"I was listening." Again he was infuriatingly calm, his voice almost gentle.

Charlie stopped struggling then and let herself relax against her husband's chest. She felt his chin come to rest on the top of her hat and wished for the first time ever that she wasn't wearing it.

"What am I going to do with you, Sean Donovan?" Charlie asked with a sigh. "You're polite to everyone, even your enemies."

"Had he physically attacked you, Charlotte, I would have knocked him across the street, but that was nothing more than the pitiful rambling of a drunk." Sean's voice was compassionate, and Charlie was more confused than ever.

Charlie turned in her husband's arms, which had loosened to allow her room. She tipped her head back and tried to see him in the now complete darkness.

"What am I going to do with you, Sean?" This time the words were whispered, and the answer was just as soft.

"I'm sure you'll think of something."

Without further words Charlie pushed away from her husband's embrace. Sean let her go, but was more than a little tempted to pull her back. He followed her home in silence, but until he fell asleep much later, his mind dwelt on how lovely she had been to hold.

twenty-three

I can't be falling for her. It's too soon." Sean had been repeating these words to himself for days, and still he was no closer to being convinced than the first time he had said them.

A week had gone by since Charlie had tried to kick Murphy. Charlie's dress had not been quite ready, so she hadn't mentioned going to church again. And even though Sean wanted very much to be in the house of the Lord, his mind was so full of his wife that attending services seemed less important right then.

All Sean had been able to do for the first few days of his marriage was thank God he was alive. But soon he had begun to notice the woman to whom he found himself married. Never in his wildest dreams did he expect her to be a woman who possessed so many of the qualities he admired.

That her life had been no bed of roses was obvious in many ways. She rarely asked for help or allowed Sean to wait on her. She never complained about the hard work or mentioned the past, but there were times when Sean would help her in some small way and immediately find himself under her scrutiny. She would stare at him as though figuring out what type of man he was, was the most important thing on earth.

Sean found himself speculating on Charlie's grandfather a good deal of the time, since he had clearly played such a large part in who Charlie had become. He'd had a good head for business, that much Sean knew, but what had he been like as a person? Sean was unaware both of the new insight he would gain and how swiftly it would come.

The day had flown by as usual, and Sean spent some extra time at the well cleaning up for supper. He knew that Charlie would have the table prepared and the meal set out by the time he arrived. He planned to mention the primer when they did the dishes.

They talked about the customers they'd had that day and even laughed about Sean getting stepped on by a workhorse.

"You can laugh," he teased her. "You weren't the one whose foot was being crushed by a thousand pounds of horse."

"He looked so comfortable too," Charlie said, her eyes lighting. "As if he could have stood there all day."

"He probably didn't even know my foot was down there."

"That's true. There's not a malicious bone in Tiny's body."

"Who in the world named him Tiny?" Sean asked as he pictured the gigantic animal in his mind. Tiny's hoofs were the size of large dinner plates.

"His owner is quite a character. He has a goat he milks every day whose name is George Washington, and a male dog named Dolly Madison."

They shared the light moment together, and then rose to clean up. It was Sean's turn to dry the dishes. He waited only until Charlie handed him the first plate before he brought up the book.

"Charlotte, I want to talk to you about the school primer." She looked startled, and Sean went on in a very gentle voice. "If you want me to return it, I will, but first I want to tell you something."

"No, I don't think that's a good idea." Charlie's voice was one of near panic.

"Charlotte," Sean called after her as she darted out of the kitchen and down the hall. With the drying cloth still in his hand, he followed.

Charlie would have shut her bedroom door, but Sean came through behind her and made the action impossible. She never dreamed he would follow her, and quickly looked about for something to do. She couldn't pick up a catalog and pretend to read, because he knew she couldn't. She didn't sew very well, so mending was out. Charlie settled on rearranging her dresser drawers.

"Charlotte, I just want to talk with you," Sean said from his place near the dresser where he'd followed her, the drying cloth now thrown over his shoulder. "I'm not trying to make you feel bad because you can't read, and if you'll just look at me for a moment I can tell you what I have in mind."

Frustration rose up in Sean as he was *completely* ignored for the first time in his adult life. He knew that if Charlie would just let him explain, the whole matter could be settled.

"Charlotte!" Sean's voice thundered in frustration, and Charlie jumped before turning to face him.

She looked up into his face with a startled kind of fear, and Sean felt more upset than ever, this time with himself. He had scared her, and that was the last thing he wanted. He suddenly raised an agitated hand to his hair, raking his fingers along his scalp. It took no more than a moment to see that his wife had flinched and was steeling herself for a blow.

Sean became utterly still. With his hand still resting on the top of his head, he saw Charlie realize her mistake and try to cover it. She straightened the front of her blouse and touched the rim of her hat as though nothing out of the ordinary had happened.

"You thought I was going to hit you." Sean's voice was strained and filled with pain.

"No, I didn't," Charlie lied.

"Yes, you did."

"No, I didn't," Charlie said, turning away sharply as she spoke. "Don't be foolish." But there was no conviction in her tone, and Sean watched as she went back to work on her dresser.

His next actions were those of a man who felt like he was going down for the third time. He would not leave this room until things were settled between them.

He found his hand gently encircling Charlie's upper arm as he reached for her. He brought her away from the dresser to stand before him, holding her there with both hands on her arms. Charlie looked up at him for a moment and then lowered her head, her hat hiding her face from Sean's view.

"Please take your hat off."

Charlie looked up, startled once again, but did as he asked.

"Look at me, Charlotte," Sean implored her softly and waited for her to comply.

Charlie had never seen a man look the way Sean looked at that moment. His face was a mask of tender determination, and she hoped he couldn't see the tears she felt gathering behind her eyes.

"I want you to listen to me, Charlotte, and listen well. I would *never* hit you. Do you hear me, Charlotte? *Never!*"

Sean watched her eyes carefully and waited until she nodded ever so slightly. Then without permission he pulled her against his chest. Cuddling her full against him, he settled his hands on her back, one thumb stroking idly along her shoulder blade. When he felt her arms come around his waist, albeit tentatively, he began to talk.

"My mother was a teacher. My oldest sister also taught before she started having children, and my younger sister has planned on becoming a teacher for as long as I can remember. I've always taken my reading skills for granted, but there were times when I think they saved my life.

"When we lived in Hawaii there was never enough to read. After coming to San Francisco and living with my Aunt Maureen, I learned what it was like to have a daily newspaper. I've always loved to read, and when I wasn't eating or out seeing the city, I could be found in my aunt's library, reading anything I could get my hands on.

"Then my mother died and my father left for the islands. I remember my sisters and I devoured every word of every newspaper available. I think the pain of my mother's death would have overwhelmed me if I hadn't had something to do with my mind. I wasn't trying to forget her, but dwelling on her loss wasn't doing me any good either. So I read.

"Rarely was a page turned that I didn't thank my mother, because she was the one who taught me to read. And Charlotte, I want to teach you."

Sean's hands slid back to her upper arms and he held her before him so he could look into her eyes.

"I want to open the world of words to you, Charlotte, because I think everyone should know how to read, and because there isn't a more precious gift *I* could give you in all the earth."

"What if I'm too stupid to learn?"

"There's nothing stupid about you."

Sean spoke with such sincerity that Charlie blinked. She did pick up on things rather quickly, but she had never stayed in school long enough to know if she could learn to read. Her grandfather had felt it unnecessary. *You know your numbers, Charlie, and enough words to get by. That's all I've ever learned. It's enough,* he used to say.

"Will you let me teach you to read?"

The question jerked Charlie back to the present, and before she could change her mind, she nodded her head. Sean grinned and pulled her into his arms again. After giving her a tender squeeze, he took her hand and led her back through the kitchen and into the living room, ignoring the unfinished dishes.

A mere moment went by before he had lit the lamp, retrieved the primer, and settled with her on the sofa. Sean read to her from the front of the book and then showed her the letters printed within.

Charlie didn't catch everything he said because she was so busy looking at him. She didn't know that men like Sean Donovan existed.

The talk around town is that you're falling for your husband. Those had been Duncan's words and Charlie felt something almost painful squeeze around her heart at the sight of this man beside her. She also found herself thinking, *the talk around town is true.*

twenty-four

Sean discovered during their second lesson that Charlie had learned the alphabet. She looked so pleased with herself that he wanted to kiss her. When he began teaching her sounds, Sean made a point of starting with words that were pertinent in her world.

While most people learned that *A* is for apple and *B* is for boy, Charlie learned that *A* is for anvil, *B* is for bellows, and *C* is for carriage.

Charlie was as fast a learner as he had expected her to be. The first few days were great, so great, in fact, that Sean was a little confused when Charlie did not want to study on their third night.

"I need to go to Sadie's," she explained, hoping that Sean would not question her.

Sean didn't question her, but he did feel let down. She seemed almost as skittish and hesitant as she had been before they'd talked. It never occurred to him that she was harboring a secret. He was quiet as they made their way to Sadie's, and just as silent as he took his place at the kitchen table. Charlie glanced at him before going to find her aunt. Sean would have been surprised to know she was laden with guilt.

"Why do you look so down?" Sadie asked as soon as Charlie stepped into the small parlor.

"I just feel bad about leaving Sean in the kitchen."

"Well, tell him to come in here and get settled then. We'll measure your dress in the sewing room."

"Is it really ready for me to try on?" Charlie asked, excitement lighting her face.

"It sure is, honey, and I'm sorry I didn't have it ready for you last week."

"It's all right, Sadie; I'm sure the dress will be worth the wait."

"So you think you'll go to church this Sunday?"

"Sean and I haven't talked about it, but I think we'll try the church that Duncan and Lora attend."

"Good," Sadie said emphatically. "Now get Sean in here so we can get to work in the sewing room. I'll have the dress ready for you to take home when you come for your bath Saturday night."

❏ ❏ ❏

Charlie could do nothing more than stare. Sadie had hurried her into the dress, made a few measurements, and whipped it back over her head before she could even think. Now the dress was hanging again, and Charlie stood before it and looked her fill.

The fabric was an off-white, almost a cream, with the palest of flowers and leaves swirled throughout in a delicate pattern. The only word that would come to Charlie's mind was "soft." The pink and blue flowers, and the green leaves and vines were all soft pastels. The small redhead reached out reverently to touch the fabric.

The sleeves were short and sewn to puff at the shoulders. The waist was gently gathered, and Charlie's hands went to her hips as she remembered the way the fabric fell in a flattering line from her waist.

"Well, what have we here?"

Charlie stiffened at the sound of Tansy's voice.

"My," Tansy said brightly, "what pretty material. I think the neckline is a little too high for my tastes, but then it's probably just right for your figure."

Wishing that Sadie hadn't left the room, Charlie watched as Tansy's shoulders went back to best display her full chest.

"Is Sean here?" Tansy did nothing to disguise the hope in her voice, and Charlie nodded reluctantly.

The voluptuous girl shot out of the room, and Charlie, after another look at her dress, followed slowly. She knew the exact moment Tansy found Sean because her voice went up three octaves in a way she thought men found attractive.

Charlie entered the small parlor to find Sean standing behind the chair and Sadie sitting on the sofa. Tansy was in front of the chair talking to Sean. His look was guarded.

"Why Sean, if I didn't know better I'd think you didn't like me." Her full lips went into a pout, and Charlie watched Sadie's eyes narrow.

"Would it help if I had Sadie make me a dress like the one she's making Charlie?"

Sean's eyes swung to his wife as Charlie, looking utterly crestfallen, turned and walked stiffly from the room.

So that's why we're over here, Sean thought. *Sadie is making a dress for my wife, and Tansy just let the cat out of the bag.* He knew it was time to put the situation in order. He came back around to the front of the chair and stood in front of Tansy. When she put one hand on his chest he removed it none too gently.

The stunning blonde looked with genuine confusion at the man before her and then took a step back.

"I'm a happily married man, Tansy," Sean's voice was implacable, "and you'll do well to remember that. Do not touch me or flirt with me again. I won't put up with it."

Tansy misunderstood, and a sly smile lit her face. "Afraid you won't be able to control yourself?"

"Exactly," Sean said sternly, only to finish by dashing Tansy's hopes. "I've never hit a woman before, and I really don't ever care to, but no one is going to hurt my wife, physically or emotionally, and get away with it."

Tansy looked around in surprise to see that Charlie had left the room. She stared uncomprehendingly at Sean and then Sadie.

"I never meant any harm, Sadie; Charlie knows that."

"No she doesn't, Tansy." Sadie's voice was the angriest Tansy had ever heard. "You've spent a lot of years playing games with men, and Charlie's never done anything but work. Now she has a man and a chance for some happiness of her own, and you're trying to take that away from her. You oughta be ashamed."

The younger woman was dispirited. She carefully turned her face away from Sean as she asked Sadie if she could still room with her.

"If you stay away from my niece's husband," Sadie answered, her voice softening some when she saw the look of regret on her boarder's face.

Sadie was still looking out the door that Tansy exited when Sean kissed her cheek. Her head whipped around in surprise to find Sean grinning at her.

"Thanks, Sadie," he said before going in search of his wife.

"You're welcome," Sadie breathed, even though he was already out of earshot. She sat thinking that if Sean Donovan wasn't married to her niece, Tansy still wouldn't stand a chance. She'd go after him herself.

◻ ◻ ◻

Charlie stood up from the back steps the moment Sean came out the door. She led the way home and didn't speak or even look at her husband. In fact, she would have gone straight to her room if Sean's voice hadn't stopped her in the hallway.

"I'm a married man, Charlotte, and where I come from that means commitment."

Charlie stopped outside her door and stared at Sean, who stood flooded in the moonlight that came through her bedroom window.

"It's nice if two people are in love, but marriage has to be built on more, or it won't last through the hard times. Even if I found Tansy attractive, which I don't, I'm committed to you and to this marriage."

Sean didn't wait for his wife to reply or even acknowledge his statement before he went into his own bedroom and shut the door.

Charlie looked at that door for a long time before closing her own to prepare for bed. She tried to relax, but she couldn't dispel the idea that Sean would never *really* be hers because he wasn't there by choice.

twenty-five

Charlie went to the post office first thing Saturday morning. No one ever wrote to her, since she had no family or friends outside of Visalia, but since Sean had been in touch with his family, she checked the mail every few days. Today there was not just a letter, but a *box* for P. Sean Donovan III. Charlie had to stop herself from running back to the livery.

Sean was intent on his work when Charlie arrived, and not wanting to startle him or cause an accident, Charlie waited for him to notice her. When he finally glanced her way, she raised the box excitedly, telling him he'd received a package.

Charlie turned and walked over to put the box on their lunch table. Sean followed her, and Charlie stood back while he worked over the string. She watched as he unwrapped a book. It took her a moment to realize that it was a Bible.

Any words that Charlie might have uttered deserted her as she watched Sean lift the book to his chest. He held it in his arms like the cherished possession that it was. His eyes were shut, and Charlie watched as a single small tear slid out one corner.

Only a minute or two passed before Sean composed himself and sat down to read the letter he found inside, but Charlie could have sworn it had been an eternity. The sight of her husband hugging his Bible and crying would be imprinted on her mind for the rest of her years.

What was in this Bible that Sean found so dear, or was it just that he had heard from his family? It was a question that hung in Charlie's mind even as she sat on the crate next to her husband and waited until he was finished reading.

❑ ❑ ❑

My dearest Sean,

There are no words to describe how we felt about your letter. You can imagine how we've prayed and longed to see you. I can't think straight when I imagine you with a rope around your neck. We would love to meet Charlotte and thank her for your life. (We thank God too.) If I understand you correctly, you didn't know Charlotte before you were married. Is that right? Please tell me more when you write back.

Marcail is working on a letter to you, and in fact it might arrive before this package. I took the liberty of sending your Bible; I knew you would want it.

You were so young when you left here that it's hard to envision you married. Is there anyone else who could watch the livery so you could both come to Santa Rosa for a visit? We would love to have you for as long as you could stay.

Gretchen and Molly are doing well—in fact everyone is on their feet except me. I'm still resting from having miscarried a baby. It was hard to lose this baby. We were so excited about him, and even though I was only three months along, this tiny infant was already a part of my heart. I know, however, that God's will is perfect. There have been tears, but Rigg and I are comforted in the fact that all through Scripture we read that our God is a righteous and fair God. Knowing this, we believe with all our hearts that this unborn baby is with Him.

What is Visalia like? Is your work steady? Have you found a Bible-preaching church? As you can see, I'm full of questions. I wish we could meet face to face and catch up. Bill, May, Jeff, and Bobbie all send their love. They're also joining us in prayer for Charlotte's salvation. I won't mention this again, so you won't fear Charlotte reading your letters, but know that we are praying.

I love you, Sean, and pray for you always.

Until next time,
Katie

❑ ❑ ❑

Drained after reading the letter, Sean wondered for a moment why Katie had made no mention of his father. He suddenly became conscious of his wife sitting beside him, and even more conscious of a headache coming on, possibly due to holding his tears in check.

"Were they glad to hear from you?"

"Yes," Sean answered and turned his head to look at her. "They wish they could meet you. In fact, they invited us for a visit if someone could watch the livery."

Charlie's mouth dropped open. "But they don't even know me."

"That doesn't matter. You're my wife, and they love you."

Charlie turned away from her husband's penetrating look. She stared across the livery at nothing and then spoke in a whisper.

"I'm sorry you can't see your family, but there's no one who could—"

She broke off when Sean's hand moved under her chin. He tenderly grasped her jaw and urged her to look at him. Her gaze was one of apology and regret.

"I didn't mean to insinuate that we should pack up and go to Santa Rosa," Sean said. "I just thought you'd like to know that my family is eager to meet you. I'll have to explain to them that due to the conditions that the judge explained, I can't leave town for five years."

Charlie nodded, and Sean gently caressed her chin with his thumb before he rose and went back to work.

◻ ◻ ◻

San Francisco

"Rigg!" Maureen Kent gasped when she saw the man her servant had just announced. "What are you doing here?"

"Have I missed Patrick?" Rigg asked about his father-in-law.

"No, he doesn't sail until morning. What's happened?"

"Rigg!"

Before Rigg could answer, Patrick Sean Donovan II had come down from upstairs and joined his sister and son-in-law in the library.

"I'm glad I didn't miss you, Patrick," Rigg breathed with relief, seeing that his presence had upset them. "We received news about Sean after you left."

Patrick sat down hard on the nearest chair, his face draining of color.

"I knew you were going to be here a few weeks before you sailed, and if I'd missed you I'd never have forgiven myself for not sending a telegram—but I wanted to come in person. Then Katie suffered a miscarriage, so I couldn't leave right away."

"Oh, Rigg," Maureen began, but he cut her off gently.

"She's all right. The doctor just wants her to rest."

Rigg stood for a moment, feeling like he needed to catch his breath.

"I have a letter, but I think I should warn you—"

"Is he alive?" the older man cut him off, his voice hoarse.

"Yes."

"Then nothing else matters."

Rigg passed the letter to Patrick and waited while he read. As soon as he had read it silently, he read it aloud to his sister, who cried in her handkerchief for some minutes. The room was silent until Maureen contained herself. Then Rigg spoke.

"Is there anything I can do?"

"Yes," Patrick replied. "You can come with me to tell the captain of the *Silver Angel* that I won't need passage, and then to the stage office so I can buy a ticket for Visalia."

twenty-six

In the beginning was the Word, and the Word was with God, and the Word was God. The same was in the beginning with God."

Sean could only read the first two verses from the book of John before his eyes filled with tears. He knew Charlie had supper on the table, but he felt an urgency to spend a few moments in God's Word. He bowed his head and prayed before he left the room. Sean thanked God for his life, his wife, and his family before his mind swung back to Charlotte and dwelt there.

"I don't know if this is love, God," he whispered, "but I care for her so much. Please help Charlotte to understand that she needs to know Your Son personally. Please save her and use us to Your glory."

The moment these words were out of his mouth, Sean envisioned them leaving for Hawaii. He stood from his kneeling place next to the bed and gazed out the window like a man in a trance.

"Back to Hawaii! Oh, God," Sean cried softly, "could that thought be from You, because nothing would make me happier than for me to return to Hawaii with Charlotte, so we could work with Father."

Sean took a moment more to give his future to God and in doing so felt an indescribable peace fall over him. He knew he couldn't tell Charlie how he felt, but he also knew that if the thought *had* come from the Lord, then He would work it out.

"Sean," Charlie called from outside the door. He'd taken more time than he thought. He opened the door to see her waiting in the hall.

"Are you all right?"

"I'm fine, Charlotte. I was reading my Bible. Did I keep you long?"

"No, but I did wonder what had happened to you. Sadie expects us for baths tonight, and I'm tired. I'd like to get over there and home before it gets too late."

Charlie talked as she led the way to the supper table where the young couple sat down and ate. Their conversation was light. Then over dishes, Charlie brought up a subject that nearly made Sean drop the plate he was drying.

"I think we should go to church in the morning."

Sean didn't answer for a moment, and Charlie turned from the dishpan to look at him. "What do you think?"

"I'd like that, Charlotte, if you're sure."

"I'm sure. I think we should go to Duncan and Lora's church."

"That sounds fine." *Fine* was not the way Sean was feeling. Ecstatic, overjoyed, or elated better described his mood, but he wasn't sure he would be able to explain himself to Charlie if he suddenly began to do handstands in the kitchen.

Ten minutes later they were on their way to Sadie's, and Charlie asked if Sean's family was well.

"They're doing pretty well. I should have read the letter to you over supper."

"You don't mind if I know what's in the letter?" Charlie seemed surprised.

"Not at all. In fact, I'll read it to you when we get home."

Charlie didn't reply, but she was so pleased she wanted to laugh just for the pleasure of it. Sean's family sounded wonderful, and he didn't seem at all hesitant to share them with her. She wouldn't trade Sadie for royalty, but for some reason, Sean's family was fascinating to her.

And the fascination only grew when they returned home and Sean read the letter. Charlie thought the names Gretchen and Molly were beautiful, and she felt terrible over Kaitlin's losing her baby.

Sean made no mention of Charlie's salvation, and so the letter just read that the family was praying for her. Charlie had never had anyone say that to her, and even though she told herself she really didn't believe in such things, the thought warmed her spirit.

Charlie was still thinking on everything Sean had said when he told her he would feed the animals in the morning. She thanked him rather absently and took herself off to bed. Imaginary visions of how Kaitlin, Marcail, Gretchen, and Molly might look filled her head as sleep overtook her.

twenty-seven

The next morning Charlie spent over 40 minutes with her dress and hair, and for a woman who usually dressed in five minutes, this was quite a task.

Sean's back was to the hallway when she entered the kitchen. Already regretting her last-minute decision to leave her hat behind, Charlie had just decided to return for it when Sean turned.

Sean had not heard her come into the room. He had been flipping pancakes, and it had taken a moment for him to realize he wasn't alone. He turned unsuspectingly with a ready smile and a morning greeting for his wife, but the words died in his throat.

Charlie's hair was swept up on top of her head in a loose bun that allowed wispy little curls to fall around her neck and forehead. Sean's eyes traveled from her slender white neck to the hem of her flowered dress and then swung back to her face. In those seconds he took in her slim waist, small breasts, and gently rounded hips. She was so utterly feminine that Sean was speechless.

"The pancakes are burning," Charlie whispered softly, having stood silent for his inspection.

Sean spun back to the stove, relieved to have a diversion. *She's darling*, he said to himself, *and she's* my *darling*.

Charlie took a place at the table and waited for Sean to join her. Sean ate his meal without once looking at his plate. Charlie's face was flushed with embarrassment and something else she couldn't quite define.

"You look very beautiful," Sean said at the end of the meal, easily holding her gaze with his own.

"Thank you." Charlie was so pleased by his words that she felt tears sting her eyes and looked swiftly down at her coffee cup.

When it was time to leave for church, it seemed to Charlie the most natural thing in the world to have Sean hitch up the buggy and help her up to her seat, an act she had never before let him perform. She felt like a lady for the first time in her life as Sean held the reins loosely in his grip and drove the buggy from the livery.

"I haven't been in church since I was a child. I'm not sure I'm going to like this."

"What has you worried?" Sean asked her softly, always alert when she spoke of her life before they met.

"Churches are full of hypocrites."

"Give me an example."

"Well, you know, when you see a man in church on Sunday and then watch him stagger out of one of the town bars on Tuesday night."

"You've seen that happen?"

"No, I guess I haven't, but I hear things."

"Charlotte," Sean asked as he realized his wife's fears were causing her judgmental remarks. "Have you ever been to this church?"

"No," she said softly. She didn't have anything more to say, but fear was closing her throat and she couldn't have spoken had she tried.

❏ ❏ ❏

"Charlotte, try to relax," Sean bent close and whispered in his wife's ear.

"I am relaxed."

Sean smiled at her reply. Her hands were clenched so tightly in her lap that her knuckles were white. The last song had been sung, and the minister was now at the front of the church behind a small pulpit for the sermon.

The Donovans were seated alone in a rear pew, and Sean was thankful for the privacy. He reached for one of her hands and brought it to the bench between them, where it was nearly hidden by the fullness of Charlie's dress.

Her hand was swallowed up by his own and ice cold. Something in Sean's heart turned over. Not that this was an unfamiliar sensation; his heart had been doing funny things for a week. Sean never dreamed a man could feel this way about a woman, and his hand tightened thinking how *right* hers felt within his own.

His thoughts were cut off when the sermon began. He took a quick peek at his wife and saw that she was attentive, and not as tied up in knots as she had been.

"I'm going to read this morning from John, chapter 3. Feel free to follow along in your own copy of God's Word. 'There was a man of the Pharisees, named Nicodemus, a ruler of the Jews; the same came to Jesus by night, and said unto him, "Rabbi, we know that thou art a teacher come from God; for no man can do these miracles that thou doest, except God be with him." Jesus answered, and said unto him, "Verily, verily, I say unto thee, except a man be born again, he cannot see the kingdom of God."'

"I need to stop here and tell you what I know about this man Nicodemus. As it says here in verse one, he was a man of the Pharisees. This was a sect of men who lived by a very strict code of laws. And the biggest problem wasn't the fact that it was impossible to obey all these laws, but that even if they could have obeyed them to the letter, it would not have saved them.

"Nicodemus must have been one of the few to see the fallacy of the Pharisee's laws. He'd certainly heard of Jesus Christ and the miracles He was able to perform, and his heart must have been hungry to know Him better.

"I find it interesting to note that Nicodemus went to Jesus by night. It's speculation on my part, but I wonder whether Nicodemus was afraid to be seen going to Jesus, or whether he felt an urgency to know the truth and couldn't wait until morning. You see, I don't believe that he doubted that this was God's Son. I know that in the Scripture Nicodemus just says God is *with* Jesus, but Nicodemus is no fool. I believe he understood that he was talking to Jesus the Christ, God's holy Son.

"I want to talk with you more about this passage of Scripture. I want you to know what the Bible has to say about Jesus Christ in the weeks to come. But before I run out of time, I must stop and ask you this: When was the last time you talked to Jesus Christ as Nicodemus did?

"We can't stand face to face with Jesus as he was able to do, but let me tell you, friends, we *can* talk to Christ as though He were in the room. I'm referring to prayer. Maybe you think praying is just for preachers, but I assure you it's not. God wants to hear from each and every one of you. First, He wants to hear you pray and give yourself to Him, or as Jesus said to be 'born again,' as we must do if we want to have eternal life. Then He wants to hear you praise Him and share your every need.

"I'm going to close with my favorite verses in all of Scripture, and they are in the same passage we are in today. John 3:16 and 17 say, 'For God so loved the world that he gave his only begotten Son, that whosoever believeth in him should not perish, but have everlasting life. For God sent not his Son into the world to condemn the world, but that the world through him might be saved.'

"If there is any doubt in your mind as to what those verses mean, please come and see me. Don't let another day pass without settling your eternity. You can know this Jesus Christ as your own personal Lord and Savior."

The congregation was dismissed with a song and then a brief prayer. Sean and Charlie stood and moved toward the door of the church. Sean was unsure what type of welcome he would receive, and afraid that if Charlie saw him rebuffed it would only confirm her belief that some of these people were hypocrites. Sean knew from firsthand experience that born-again Christians were not perfect, and he understood that they might be quite hesitant to associate with a convicted bank robber.

Sean convinced himself that leaving quickly was the best answer to protecting his wife's feelings. They were halfway to the buggy when Duncan called out. Sean and Charlie both turned to see Visalia's sheriff and his wife approaching, each wearing huge smiles of welcome.

twenty-eight

It's great to see you here, Sean." Duncan spoke softy while Lora took Charlie over to meet her daughter and grandson.

"It's great to be here," Sean cheerfully replied, grabbing Duncan's hand.

"How are things going at home and in the livery?"

"Unbelievably. Charlotte treats me like a king."

Duncan nodded. "I knew you would do well together. I'm sure you've caught on that her growing-up years were not easy."

"She doesn't share much, but it's obvious."

"Have you had a chance to talk about spiritual things?"

"Not really. I mean, she's somewhat open when we talk, but I think she's afraid to ask too many questions; fearful of intruding into my past. And I'm wary of pushing her and saying too much."

"I can understand that. We'll keep praying, Sean."

"Thanks, Duncan. I want you to know that my main prayer is that Charlotte will come to Christ. God has already answered so many prayers in my life, so quickly, and I really do understand that oftentimes He asks us to wait. I was saved from hanging, and just minutes later I was married. Now in a very short time I've come to care deeply for my wife.

"My deepest desire is that Charlotte will be saved and we'll go to Hawaii someday to continue the mission work there. It's not going to happen overnight, like it has so far, but God is sufficient, and I know that in His time, we'll be wherever He leads."

Duncan reached out and touched the younger man's shoulder. He seemed unable to speak, and Sean, who turned to watch his wife some ten yards away, was glad for the silence.

❑ ❑ ❑

Sean lay in bed Sunday night and reflected on the day. There had been nothing but handshakes and smiles of welcome from the pastor and the rest of the congregation. Duncan and Lora had even asked them to dinner, but Charlie had explained with visible regret that her Aunt Sadie was expecting them.

Lora, in her gracious, unpretentious manner, simply asked the Donovans to come the following week, and Charlie had quickly accepted. Sean wondered if anyone had ever tried to reach out to Charlie in the past, or if someone had tried and been rejected. He also wondered how much of this she was doing for him. He felt grateful over this thought, but also prayed that Charlie would soon have an interest in eternal issues.

For the first time he understood the way his sister must have felt as she watched him grow harder and harder toward God. Kaitlin had known that Sean's eternity was secure, while Sean didn't have the same assurance about Charlie's, but that wouldn't stop the ache, the longing, to have your loved one walk in the way of the Lord.

Sean fell asleep thinking about his father. Had he ever made it back to Santa Rosa? Evidently not, since Katie hadn't even mentioned him in her letter. Sean tried not to read anything into that, but he knew in an instant that he was not completely over his anger. Within seconds his mind was immersed in his painful past. How long would Father stay away? How long before he would see that his family needed him? How long before things could be patched up between father and son?

If only we could be in touch, even in a letter. Those were Sean's last thoughts before he remembered he'd written back to his sister just that evening and asked about Father. Now all he could do was wait, or hope that Marcail's letter would arrive with some news.

❏ ❏ ❏

"Do you believe what that preacher said on Sunday about prayer?"

Sean sighed with relief over the question. Charlie had been very quiet since Sunday morning, and Sean simply didn't know how to ask her what she was thinking. It was Wednesday, and they were relaxing in the living room of their small home as the sun sank low in the sky.

"Yes, I believe it. Is there something in particular you're questioning?"

Charlie looked embarrassed and then quietly admitted, "I'm not really sure there's even Someone up there, let alone talking as though God was in the same room with me."

"Why don't you think God exists?"

Charlie shrugged. "He never answered my prayers when I was young, so I knew He wasn't there and just stopped praying."

Sean wasn't sure what to say. He believed that God's will was perfect, even when it hurt, but how did you explain that to someone whose faith was nonexistent?

"What types of things did you pray about?" Sean felt he had picked a safe question and was certain when a smile came over his wife's face.

"I wanted a pony of my very own," Charlie sighed. "All the horses were always so big for me, and I wanted one I could mount and ride on my own. But a pony wouldn't have been an asset to the business, so Grandpa said no."

Sean was quiet, hoping that she would continue. He never suspected that his feelings, already very protective, would forever deepen in their intensity.

"I also asked God to make my grandfather stop hitting me." Charlie didn't look at Sean as she continued, "It seemed that I couldn't do anything right when I was growing up, and Grandpa's answer was always an open-handed blow. Sadie said it wasn't me, that he was just like that. He used to slap her all the time too.

"Sadie also believes that he hit my mother so hard that she died having me. My mother would never tell him who my father was, and even though she'd always been his favorite child, Grandpa wouldn't forgive her.

"Sadie married Harry just to get away from Grandpa, and they had a good life together. They even tried to take me in, but Grandpa fell in love with my red hair. Even though he acted like he hated me half of the time, he wouldn't let me go."

Charlie had stared out the window for this emotionless recital, and Sean couldn't take his eyes from her. How could anyone have mistreated this girl? How could anyone have laid a violent hand on this woman? They were sharing the sofa, and an instant later, Sean, overcome with his newfound emotions, covered the distance that separated them and took his wife in his arms.

Charlie whispered in his ear as she let him hold her close, "I'm all right, Sean."

"Well, I'm not," he whispered back and settled her head more comfortably on his shoulder. "I'm not going to let anyone else hurt you."

His hold was almost crushing her, but Charlie didn't resist. After a few moments she sighed, "It was all a long time ago." She sounded very reasonable. "You are really too sensitive, you know, and I don't know what I'm going to do with you."

Sean didn't answer. He pressed his lips to her forehead and his arms tightened slightly. Charlie turned her head to look up into his face, glad that she was once again without her hat. Sean's eyes traveled caressingly over her features and emotions flooded through him, ranging from fierce protectiveness to tender desire.

He realized in that instant that he was truly in love with this woman. He ached to declare his love for her, but a tiny fear of rejection lingered in his mind. The desire to kiss her was overpowering, and almost of its own volition his head began to lower. His lips were just a breath away from Charlie's when a knock sounded at the front door.

Sean drew back reluctantly. He rose from the sofa, but the look of longing on his wife's face made him sit back down and reach for her. The knock sounded again.

"Later," Sean said in a strained voice as he once again pulled away. "We'll finish this later."

The sun was still casting an orange glow in the sky as Sean answered the summons at the door. There wasn't much light, and the man at the door was now a stranger, but Sean knew him. His face was older, and he looked thinner than the boy of 14 remembered, but Sean would have known his father anywhere.

twenty-nine

Patrick felt as if the air had been knocked from his body at the sight of his son. He had left a frightened 14-year-old boy and come back to find a man, strong of limb and features. In fact, he felt like he was looking at a younger version of himself.

"Hello, Sean." The older man spoke softly.

Sean was silent as he moved back and held the door for his father to enter. Patrick stepped across the threshold and stood with his hat in his hand. Sean made no move to touch him, and the two men stood in the lantern light eyeing one another. Sean wished he could say just one of the things he had rehearsed while he waited for this man. Patrick was also quiet, not wanting to say anything that might drive an even bigger wedge between them.

Charlie, curious about the silence in the kitchen, came from the living room and stood beside her husband. Patrick's gaze swung to the small redhead and he smiled in relief.

"You must be Charlotte?" he guessed. Setting his small bag down, Patrick held out his hand. Charlie was quick to offer her hand to this stranger, having weighed the situation up in an instant. "I'm Patrick Donovan, Sean's father."

"It's nice to meet you," Charlie offered sincerely.

"How did you know this was Charlotte?" Sean asked, speaking his first words.

"I was just in Santa Rosa for a visit, and then I was at your aunt's with plans to sail when Rigg showed up with your letter."

"This is your first visit back then?"

"No, actually it isn't," Patrick said somewhat reluctantly. "I was back two years ago, but when I arrived in Santa Rosa, Katie told me I'd missed you by about six weeks."

"*Six weeks*," Sean said the words in a stunned whisper as pain crowded in around his chest. After a moment he seemed to mentally shake himself. "Well, come in and have a seat. Are you hungry?"

"Thank you, no."

Once in the living room, Charlie and Sean took the sofa and Patrick took the chair. Again silence prevailed.

"Was it a rough trip over from San Francisco?" asked Charlie.

"Not bad," Patrick smiled at his daughter-in-law for the lifeline she had tossed him. "This is hot country over here, but I met some interesting people."

"You came by train?"

"For the most part. It's a good way to see the area." The remark sounded ridiculous even to his own ears, but nothing else came to mind.

"I've never been on a train," Charlie continued, thinking that the elder Mr. Donovan looked rather lost.

She wished that Sean would get involved in the conversation. He was sitting ramrod straight, his eyes taking in Charlie and his father with measured glances. Sean's face, Charlie noted, gave away none of his feelings. Charlie talked with her father-in-law for the better part of an hour before he rose.

"Well, it's been good visiting with you, but it's getting late. If you could point me in the direction of the hotel, I'll go get a room for the night." He tried to keep the disappointment from his voice.

"You don't need to stay at the hotel," Charlie said as she and Sean both stood. "We don't really have room for you, but my aunt runs a boardinghouse and I know she'd be glad to have you. It's very clean, and you would have your own room."

"Well, if you're sure it wouldn't be an imposition."

"I'm sure. Sean and I can walk you over."

It was a silent threesome that made their way to Sadie's. Sean stood with his father in the kitchen while Charlie went in search of Sadie.

"Sadie is very hospitable," Sean told his father. "Don't hesitate to ask for whatever you need."

"I won't."

Again the heavy silence fell.

"I smith for Charlotte at the livery," Sean began again. "I have to work tomorrow, but you're welcome to come by anytime."

"Thank you, Sean," Patrick responded, working again to keep the emotion from his voice. "I'll plan on that."

Sadie bustled into the room a moment later, and before following her to his room, Patrick bid his family goodnight.

Seeing how badly he needed time to adjust to his father's presence, Charlie wasted no time in getting Sean out the door and home. As soon as they were within the walls of their own home, Charlie told Sean she was going to bed.

"I'm tired, and I suspect you need some time to think." Charlie turned toward the hallway and then hesitated. "If you need to talk, Sean, just knock on my door."

"Thanks, Charlotte."

Sean waited until she had gone into her room before moving toward his own. He did need some time, she had been right about that, but what was he to do with that time? Did he pray and ask God to erase all the years of hurt and confusion, or did he walk straight back to Sadie's and confront the father he believed had deserted him and his sisters when they needed him most?

Sean opted for prayer. Not so that he could forget all the hurt, but so that he could put aside the anger and bitterness that still rode him. If he didn't, he was sure to have even more regrets after what was certain to be a brief time with his father.

◻ ◻ ◻

Why didn't you come back? Didn't you realize how much we needed you? I was so angry with you, I think I must have hated you. I can't believe you could put the work at the mission ahead of your family . . .

Sean's thoughts gave him little rest through the night. But the anger in his heart was abating, and Sean was pleased because he didn't want to face his father with angry words. The questions that came to his mind again and again, however, *had* to be answered.

One look at Sean's face the following morning, and Charlie knew just how bad his night had been; hers hadn't been much better. As soon as she had shut her door, she wished she had asked Sean to move into her bedroom. They needed each other, for love and companionship. It was impossible to say when the time would be right again. The thought saddened her.

The conversation over breakfast was subdued, and both husband and wife were glad to get into the livery to start their daily tasks. Sean was in the midst of shoeing one of their own horses when his father appeared.

Sean's back was to the stall opening, and Charlie, not wanting to break his concentration, did not alert him of his father's presence.

Patrick watched in fascination as his son worked. Katie had written about the fine blacksmith Sean had been when he was 16 and 17, but as Patrick watched Sean's capable hands, he realized that her letters didn't do him justice. Patrick also took note of Charlie, who assisted her husband with quiet efficiency. They made an ideal partnership.

He prayed silently as the couple finished, asking God as he had last night and all this morning to ease the way between Sean and himself. He knew he deserved his son's anger, but he also knew that he would go nowhere until things between them were settled. Sean had been so silent the night before that Patrick had no gauge as to how long that could take. He prayed that his emotions as well as his finances would hold.

The task complete, Sean emerged from the stall, effectively breaking into his father's thoughts. Again Patrick spoke the first words that came to mind.

"Your grandfather was a blacksmith back in Ireland, Sean. I don't know if you remember me telling you that."

"Actually, I'd forgotten," Sean's said, surprise filling his voice. Then the memories flooded back. "You helped him from the time you could walk."

"That's right, I did—right up to the day before I left for America."

An uncomfortable silence fell for the space of a few heartbeats, and then Sean began to show his father around the livery. Patrick was as impressed as Sean had been on his first day. Charlie joined them, and Sean moved from stall to stall with his arm around his wife. It was a comfort to touch her; his life with her seemed more concrete to him than being able to call this man Father.

The day was not as uncomfortable as Sean would have thought. In fact, although impersonal, the next three days were very relaxed. Patrick spelled Charlie in the livery whenever he could, and Charlie, although she missed Sean's company, left father and son alone often, knowing they needed to talk.

Charlie could have stayed without worrying. In the end, the showdown between father and son was to come at a time no one could have predicted.

thirty

════════════════

It felt very odd for Sean to be taking his father to church. He wondered at the tenseness he felt, and then realized how much he craved his father's approval of the church he attended.

As the pastor had said, they were once again studying the life of Jesus Christ. Each time Sean looked down at his own Bible, his eyes drifted to his father's lap and the Bible resting there, remembering the Christmas his mother had given it to him.

Sean had been about nine that Christmas, and very interested in boats and sailing. He simply couldn't understand why his mother was so excited to be giving her husband a new Bible. A *Bible*? Surely his father would be disappointed. To Sean's surprise, he wasn't.

On Christmas morning it was the last gift to be opened, and Sean had watched his mother sit on the edge of her chair. He had no idea how long she had waited for that Bible to arrive, praying it would be on time and undamaged.

Sean could see in an instant that his father was thrilled with his gift. He caressed the leather binding and touched the pages before turning unsuspectingly to the front where his mother had written some well-chosen words.

Sean recalled the way his father's eyes swam with tears as he looked across the room at his spouse. It was some time before Sean was able to see what his mother had written, but he knew they were words he would never forget.

> My darling Patrick,
>
> No day passes that I don't rejoice in our marriage. No month goes by that I don't see you growing in the Word. With each new year our love increases. And when at last we stand in heaven, I'll thank our eternal Father for blessing our life together here on this soil.
>
> All my love,
> Theresa

The Bible was no longer new, and the woman who had written the message had gone on before them, but her message was as powerful to Sean now as it was the first time he had read it. Sean suddenly felt overwhelmed with the loss of his mother. It wasn't really his mother's death that grieved him as much as his father's having to be alone, and how little he now knew his father because of the mistakes he had made.

With an effort Sean pulled his mind back to the present. He had missed half the sermon while his mind wandered to events of the past and things he couldn't change. There was the present and the future to think about, and in those he could play a part. It was time to talk with his father; not the small talk they'd been uttering for days, but *real* talk.

Having come to this decision, Sean remembered they were going to Duncan's for dinner. He prayed for patience over the delay, and then asked God to bless them when the timing was right.

□ □ □

The conversation over dinner was lighthearted and fun. Duncan and Lora were thrilled to meet Patrick and welcomed him into their home with all the love and graciousness that Charlie and Sean had come to expect.

The party of five was just finishing their coffee and dessert when Duncan's deputy came to the door. He said he had a problem at the office that would not wait. Duncan regretfully bid his wife and guests goodbye.

Sean and Patrick both offered to help the women with cleanup, but Lora said the kitchen was too small for so much help. She showed them into a spacious, comfortable living room and left them alone.

Patrick was silent as his gaze took in the room, and it was a few moments before he realized Sean was staring at him. Their eyes met, so alike in shape and color, and Sean finally asked the question that had been on his mind for more than five years.

"Why didn't you come back?

Patrick's eyes slid shut for just an instant, relieved that his son finally wanted to talk.

"At first, it was because they needed me, Sean."

"We needed you too."

"I know you did, but at the time, I believed they needed me more."

Sean was quiet as the remembered pain flooded back in upon him, and then he realized exactly what his father had said.

"What did you mean—at first?"

Patrick seemed reluctant then, but Sean never took his eyes from his father, forcing Patrick to take a deep breath and tell his story.

"As selfish as this is to admit, it was almost a relief to have a catastrophe on my hands the moment I returned to the islands. I was so busy for the first seven months that I had little time to miss you kids and your mother.

"But then things began to regulate. Not enough so that I felt I could leave, but enough so that I had more time on my hands—time to think about all I'd lost. The evenings were the worst. When daylight disappeared and there was nothing more I could do for the day, I'd go back to our empty little house that had miraculously survived the hurricane and sit alone until I thought I would die of loneliness, or worse yet, have to keep on living. Then the lies began."

"The lies?" Sean broke in softly, not fully believing what he was hearing.

"Yes, lies," Patrick admitted. "It was easy, you know, to lie in the letters and tell you I was doing well and praying for you. But I wasn't. I was so eaten up with bitterness that God would take my wife when I believed I needed her most that I stopped praying."

"But you continued to minister to the people there?"

"Yes, I did, and only a select few knew I was struggling. When I finally made it to Santa Rosa, Katie told me how your backsliding had been slow in coming. I couldn't help but think how alike we are.

"Not that I was happy about such a comparison, but three years had passed before I made it back to California and spiritually, I was still on shaky ground. In fact, it was in Santa Rosa that I got things straight, and in a way I have you to thank."

"Me?"

"Yes, Sean, you. When I watched your mother's health decline, I thought I'd felt as helpless as a man could, but at least I knew where she was. It was worse with you. I'm thankful that Katie spared me nothing. She told me, sometimes at the top of her voice, how disappointed she was, and how I'd missed you by only a

few weeks. I can't tell you the pain I felt to think that my
17-year-old son was out wandering the state and possibly the country, on his own. The decision to leave was
yours, Sean, but I should have returned sooner. I just
kept telling myself that I couldn't face all of you. You
thought I was a pillar of spiritual strength. In actuality, I
was a mass of pain and anger."

"I still don't understand where I came into the picture."

Patrick took a breath; remembering was painful. "The
helplessness Sean—that was my final downfall. You
were gone and I didn't know where. I had no other
choice but to call on God and give myself back to Him
completely. My despair was so great that I don't believe I
would be here today had I not done just that."

Patrick fell silent at this point, giving Sean time to
think. Of all the scenarios he had conjured up in his
mind, the idea of his father living in bitterness against
God was not one of them. But so much made sense now.
Sean could never reckon the man who left California
with a man who could leave his family for years, but now
Sean saw that it could happen.

Sean wanted to thank his father for baring his heart so
completely, but there was a little more he had to know.

"You said you had been in Santa Rosa for a visit, so I
assume you went back to Hawaii two years ago."

"Yes, I did. I stayed with Rigg and Katie for about two
months and then with Maureen for a few weeks."

"Did you take Marc with you?"

"No," Patrick smiled. "Your sister had become quite
grown up, and she told me very seriously that she wished
to remain in Santa Rosa. I felt it was for the best, so I went
back alone."

"What brought you back now?"

"Time. When I left two years ago I decided I would not

stay away for more than a two-year period, no matter what was happening on the islands."

"Were you in Santa Rosa when Kate had her miscarriage?" Sean's voice was as impersonal as it had been during the entire conversation.

"No." Patrick suddenly looked older than Sean had ever seen him. "Rigg told me when he got to Maureen's. He also told me that she deliberately kept from mentioning me in her letter to you because she didn't know if Rigg would catch me before I sailed."

"I'm glad he did." Sean spoke thickly, no longer able to hide his breaking heart.

"Are you really, Sean? Are you really glad?" Patrick's voice was desperate, and Sean saw the tears in his eyes.

Lora and Charlie planned to join the men at that moment, but the sight of Patrick and Sean embracing in the middle of the room stayed their action.

As they turned away, Lora saw the tears in Charlie's eyes and assumed they were tears of joy, as her own were. She would have been surprised to know that Charlie's tears came from believing she had just lost the most precious thing she'd ever found.

thirty-one

The next three days were a time of joy and laughter for Sean and his father. They talked almost nonstop. Sean learned of his sisters' activities and those of his beloved nieces. Aunt Maureen had sent her love also, and Sean had even taken time to write to her.

Patrick also spent time getting to know his daughter-in-law, and joined the family with renewed purpose in prayers for her salvation. But it was obvious that something had changed between husband and wife.

That Charlie was trying to give Patrick and Sean time together was clear, but she seemed to be doing so at the expense of her own marriage. Patrick said as much to Sean one evening when they were alone in the living room.

"It's time for me to go, Sean."

"So soon?"

Patrick nodded. "It is soon, but my presence is not helping your marriage, and I think that needs to be a priority right now."

Sean's face was a mask of confusion. Finally he spoke. "She seems to have drawn farther away from me every day you've been here, and yet I know she likes you."

"Have you had a chance to ask her about it, like when you retire for the night?"

Sean hesitated for only a moment. "We don't share a bedroom."

Patrick was not surprised at the lack of intimacy in the marriage. He had been happily, *intimately*, married for over 20 years himself, and he knew the signs. He had seen Sean touch Charlie, but they never looked at each other the way Rigg and Katie did—in a way that told how one found the other to be wonderful and desirable.

Patrick decided to keep most of his thoughts to himself, and when he spoke his look was kindness itself. "You're nearly strangers, Sean, but I can see she cares for you, and unless I miss my guess, you're in love with her."

"You're right. I do think I'm in love, but how can I be?" Sean voiced the question that would not leave his mind. "As you said, we're practically strangers."

"I've always believed that love can happen very fast. Believe me, love is what gives a marriage joy, but the factor that's going to stand the test of time is your—"

"Commitment," Sean finished for his father, and Patrick's eyes grew suspiciously wet.

"Yes, commitment. Some people feel this is some sort of duty, but in fact it gives a marriage very real stability." They talked for the next hour and then spent another hour in prayer.

Sean went to bed in a quandary of emotions, at peace with God and his father, but saddened to see the parent he had come to love all over again leave. He knew Patrick planned to tell Charlie the next day that he would be leaving the day after.

Suddenly Sean didn't feel quite so sad. He was more than ready to work on his relationship with his wife, and his father was right—his presence was something of a hindrance. If only he and Charlie had already come to the point of conversing as husband and wife should, Sean would have felt on more stable ground. As it was, he felt only confusion.

Charlie had constantly put Sean and his father together as though she approved of the relationship, and yet she suddenly seemed to disapprove of Sean. The smiles he had begun to see more and more frequently had disappeared altogether, and in the evenings when they had some time to work on the reading, Charlie would take herself off to her room and not come out before morning.

Sean prayed about the time he could approach Charlie, wanting desperately to lean on God for this. He fell asleep as he always did, asking God to bring his wife to a saving knowledge of Jesus Christ.

❑ ❑ ❑

"I really would like to pay you for the room and board."

"I won't even discuss it with you," Sadie told Patrick in a no-nonsense voice. "You're Charlie's father-in-law, and that makes you family. I don't charge family."

Sadie's hands were on her hips, her eyes daring Patrick to argue with her. Patrick eyed her for just a moment before he spoke graciously.

"Then I thank you, Sadie, for your hospitality."

"You're welcome," Sadie told him simply and turned away, looking for something to do with her hands. He was the most handsome man she had seen in years, and for some reason, Sadie felt a bit flustered in his presence. But flustered or not, she felt it was a pity he had to leave.

Sadie's wayward thoughts were interrupted by the arrival of Sean and Charlie. They were there to walk Patrick to the train station. Patrick, his manner once again quiet and gracious, thanked Sadie for the last time. He was unaware of the way she stood in front of the boardinghouse and watched him leave.

□ □ □

"Charlotte, I can't thank you enough," Patrick said as he pulled his daughter-in-law into his sturdy embrace. The walk to the train station had been very quiet. Charlie realized in that instant how much she'd come to care for her husband's father.

"Do you really need to leave?" she asked in all sincerity.

"I'm afraid so. Taking the afternoon train like this will make for a long evening and a sleepless night, but I really must be on my way. I'll write, and you know I'll be praying for you."

The words made Charlie feel like crying, and she nearly broke down as she watched Patrick and Sean embrace unashamedly for long moments. She moved a few yards down the platform to give them some time alone.

"I know that God is going to do mighty things in your life, Sean, and I believe one of the first will be the salvation of your wife." Patrick's voice was low, but Sean caught every word.

"I'm praying you're right."

"Pray *believing*, Sean." Patrick spoke with conviction. "God loves her more than you do, and nothing would give Him greater joy than to bring Charlotte to Himself."

Sean wondered how he'd gotten along for so many years without this man. The thought caused him to put his arms around his father once again.

The next few minutes passed in a flurry of activity as last-minute passengers boarded and the final whistle blew. Patrick hugged his beloved children one last time, and they stood waving after he boarded and until the train was out of sight.

Both husband and wife were very quiet as they headed home for the evening. They were done working for the day, but the hour wasn't at all late. Sean's thoughts turned to his marriage, and he hoped they might be able to talk as soon as they were home. Charlie, however, surprised him and put an immediate stop to any such plans.

Just as they approached the back of the livery, Sean watched Charlie veer off.

"I've got some things I need to do in the livery, Sean."

The young husband was so surprised that he didn't speak for a few seconds. "Is there something I can help with?" he finally asked.

"No," Charlie answered a little too emphatically as she moved toward the barn. "I'll be in later."

Sean didn't have a clue as to what he should say to that, so he stood still until she disappeared into the rear door of the livery. He spent a few moments in prayer before turning and going on to the house.

thirty-two

H*e'll stay*, Charlie told herself as she stood in the warm, dim barn, *but only because he has to. He'd have left today if he could have, and after seeing his father he'll probably be watching for a chance to run.* The thought caused an ache in Charlie that she would not have believed possible. It also started her tears.

As a child it had become familiar to hurt inside, knowing that her grandfather would often have liked to rid himself of her. With Sean it was much more than just hurt, it was . . .

The thought hung on like a bad headache, and Charlie's arms went around her middle, as though the pain was centered there. It wasn't. The pain was higher and squeezed around the region of her heart like a cruel fist.

She wondered during one brief moment of near insanity what Sean would do if she went back into the house and told him she was in love with him. He might go down on his knee and declare his own love and then take her in his arms. After all, he did care some; she was sure of that. And then she knew it would never happen.

"He'd laugh in your face, Charlie, and you know it."

Sean was so surprised to hear his wife's voice that it halted his progress through the back door. He had

stayed in the house until he could no longer stand it. It
had never occurred to him that she wasn't alone in the
livery. Maybe someone was trying to hurt her. It was this
thought that propelled him forward, his face a mask of
worry.

"Charlotte?" Sean blurted as soon as he spotted her in
one of the stalls, instantly feeling contrite over the way
he had startled her.

Charlie had come away from the wall of the stall
where she was leaning and was now kneeling on the
ground. She frowned when she realized she hadn't
brought her gun. After all, it could have been anyone.

Sean didn't like that frown, but he came forward anyway. Charlie watched as he lowered himself to the ground
and leaned against the wall of the stall, as she had been
doing. He just stared at her as she sat back on her heels,
her knees just inches from his outstretched legs. The
window above them lit the stall, casting a soft light
around Charlie's red hair.

"I hope that frown isn't for me."

"It's not," Charlie answered and then looked away,
knowing no matter how kind he was, she mustn't let
herself get more attached to this man than she already
was.

"Are you all right?"

"Why wouldn't I be all right?" Charlie's tone was
suspicious.

"Since you're the one who's been crying, you'll need
to tell me." Sean's voice was soft, and Charlie turned her
head slowly back to look at him. Her look was filled with
surprise, and Sean had to speculate for only a moment
on what she might be thinking.

"How did you know I'd been crying?"

Sean smiled; he couldn't help it. "Charlotte." Again
his voice was very low. "Haven't you ever looked in the

mirror after you've cried?" Sean raised one finger and tenderly touched one corner of Charlie's red-rimmed eyes.

The act was too much for the confused redhead. Her eyes filled with tears once again and before she could even draw a breath, Sean gathered her to himself.

Charlie told herself to pull away, but his arms felt so good, and he smelled wonderful. She suddenly remembered the regret on her husband's face when he realized that he had missed his father by six weeks. Knowing that he was never even supposed to be here, and that he would never really be hers, was enough to make her cry all the harder.

"Charlotte, Charlotte, please try to stop. You're going to make yourself sick." Sean stroked her hair with his free hand and thought his heart would break. If only she would confide in him. Theirs had become a strange relationship all over again. Husband and wife, but not lovers. Housemates, but just barely friends.

Charlie, in an attempt to stop her tears, drew in a shuddering breath and tipped her head back to look at her husband. She told herself to thank him and move out of his arms, but no words would come. She watched Sean's gaze drop from her eyes to her mouth, and still she couldn't move. Not even when she watched his head lower and felt his hand holding the back of her head, was she able to put any space between them.

The kiss was like nothing Sean had ever dreamed of. He honestly believed he was going slowly, but when Charlie whimpered he knew he was crushing her in his arms. He loosened his hold without breaking the kiss, shifting his wife onto his lap as he did. She was kissing him back now, and Sean felt as lightheaded as a man who had gone for days with an empty stomach.

Empty. That word perfectly described Sean's arms a moment later when Charlie suddenly pushed away from him and stood a few yards away. Sean took several deep breaths and had to clear his throat before he spoke.

"I'm not going to apologize for that, Charlotte, because saying I'm sorry would be a lie. I like kissing you, and I hope someday you'll enjoy it too."

"I enjoyed it." Charlie could have pulled her own tongue out.

"Then why are you way over there looking terrified?"

"I don't know. There's so much between us, and I think if we had continued it would have complicated things further." The words were stilted, and Sean wished with all his might that he knew what she was talking about. Complicate what things?

"Charlotte, I'm not sure I understand."

"And I'm not sure I can explain."

Sean realized he would have to be satisfied with that. He stood, determined not to press her, but equally determined not to leave her in the barn alone.

"Why don't we head inside now. Maybe we can talk some more tomorrow."

Charlie seemed relieved by his understanding and went willingly with him to the house.

❑ ❑ ❑

"While you're here I want to get a lot of this done. Everything is pretty small, and I guess that's why it has been sitting for so long. They are just the jobs I never seem to get started."

Sean listened silently as Charlie spoke over lunch. She was communicating with him now, but all was strictly business. She had also insinuated often in the last three days that Sean was going somewhere. It was always subtle, but Sean never missed it. To his surprise Charlie had been eager to resume her reading lessons. At first it made no sense, but as Sean listened to his wife, he realized she wanted him to teach her before he *left*.

Well she's going to be in for a surprise, Sean thought to himself, *because I'm not going anywhere*.

In fact, he was going to be beside her even more, as much as it was in his power to do so, and his plan of attack was going to begin that very evening.

As had become their routine since the day after Patrick left, Charlie quickly cleared the kitchen table and re-trieved the primer. She turned the lantern high and waited for Sean to join her.

"Why don't we study in the living room tonight?" Sean suggested as he picked up the lantern and pulled out his wife's chair. She looked surprised, but preceded Sean into the other room, primer in hand.

Sean sat very close to Charlie on the sofa and took the book from her grasp. He opened to the page where he wanted her to start and stayed close as she read. She was doing exceptionally well, and Sean uttered only a few corrections as she read the simple story. She stumbled over the word "ear" and Sean helped her, but before she could read on, he interrupted.

"You have very nice ears," he said softly. "I wonder why I've never noticed them before."

Charlie's hand came up. She touched her ear self-consciously, turning slightly to look at her husband. He was nearly touching her with the way he was leaning to read over her shoulder, and as soon as her eyes caught his, he winked at her.

Charlie nearly dropped the book, and Sean smiled as she cleared her throat and tried once again to read. But Sean could tell she wasn't concentrating. She stumbled over words she had never had any difficulty with, and after a few moments Sean took pity on her.

"Could we skip the reading lesson tonight, Charlotte?"

"Skip it?" Charlie's voice was several octaves higher than normal, and she looked ready to panic at the way Sean shifted even closer.

"Yes, skip it. I want to ask you something. Do you like children?"

Charlie did drop the book then. Her head turned at a nearly impossible angle to look at the man beside her. What in the world had gotten into him? Charlie wasn't really sure she wanted to know.

"I think maybe I'd like a bath tonight." Charlie's voice was breathless as she moved to get up, but Sean leaned so close that his nose was brushing her temple. She froze in her place.

"You don't need a bath. You smell wonderful."

Charlie could only gawk at her spouse.

"What happened, Charlotte?" Sean entreated softly, his face close to hers. "What happened after the last time we sat on this couch together and acted like husband and wife?"

Charlie knew exactly the evening to which he referred. It was the night Sean had been about to kiss her, and they had been interrupted by his father. She answered without looking at him.

"I'm not sure what happened, Sean, but I know your father's interrupting us was for the best."

"Why do you say that?"

"Because it's true. You don't belong with a girl like me. You belong with someone beautiful and feminine like your sisters. I can only guess at how much you miss them. I was a fool to think you'd ever really be mine."

Sean's hand gently grasped her face and turned her gaze back to his.

"Charlotte, you're my wife!" Sean's voice was urgent. "It's true that I miss my family, and it was hard to see my father leave, but this is where I belong, here with you."

"But you wish you could be elsewhere."

"Not without you," he told her simply. "Whenever I think about visiting my family, or even going to see my father in Hawaii, you're with me. The idea of leaving you behind or leaving you at all is inconceivable to me."

Charlie searched his face and learned in an instant that she had been blind to Sean's true feelings about her.

"Charlotte, will you please ask me the question that you wanted to ask me days ago?"

Charlie didn't know how he knew about that, but neither did she care. "Sean, how do you feel about sharing my room?"

Sean's smile was so tender that Charlie's breath left her in a rush. They leaned toward each other at the same time, and Sean suddenly understood the silly look Kate always had on her face after Rigg kissed her—he would have sworn he was floating.

He also knew that he could now tell Charlie he loved her, but he knew he had time—all the time in the world.

thirty-three

It took Sadie exactly five seconds to notice the new intimacy between Sean and Charlie. If there *had* been any doubt in her mind, and there wasn't, it would have been resolved when Charlie stayed in the kitchen to talk with Sean during his bath. Naturally Sadie approved wholeheartedly, and would have approved all the more had she known the whole story.

Rarely had two people been so lovingly compatible. Evening lessons with the primer were now spent in the bed they shared as husband and wife, and Sean was always ready with a kiss for a job well done.

Sean learned in no time at all that Charlie loved to have her back scratched. In fact, she was downright greedy about it! Her request for him to scratch a certain spot on her back for a minute always turned into a half-hour. She was disappointed when he stopped, even when he told her his arm was ready to fall off.

Their favorite times were Sunday mornings, because they were able to sleep in. Since the livery was closed, the only chores were feeding the stock and checking the forge. They were usually able to cuddle and talk in bed for more than an hour before they needed to get ready for church. It was during this time that they had their most important discussions.

"Sean, can I ask you something?"

"Sure."

"The night you moved into my room, you asked me if I liked children. Why?" Sean's shoulder vibrated under Charlie's cheek and jaw. "What's so funny?"

"Me," Sean answered her, his voice still full of laughter. "I couldn't for the life of me figure out how to bring the conversation around to intimate things, so I thought if we talked about babies, you'd understand that I wanted a marriage in every way and that I was *going* nowhere."

"Oh," Charlie replied thoughtfully. Sean shifted so he could see her face.

"By the way, you never answered me. *Do* you like children?"

"I think so. I haven't been around them much."

"What was your own childhood like?" It was a question Sean had wanted to ask for a long time, and he prayed even now as he waited to see if his timing had been right.

"Not much fun," Charlie admitted softly. "I could never do anything right."

"You mean in your grandfather's eyes?"

Charlie sighed. "He was not an easy man."

"Tell me about him," Sean entreated, attempting with his voice and eyes to tell her just how much he wanted to know.

"Sadie told me he'd always been the same," Charlie began. "Even when she was a little girl she remembers him being overbearing and cruel. Sadie thinks his own father must have treated him that way; it was the only way he ever knew. She also thinks it would have been better if either she or my mother had been a boy."

"You didn't know your mother, did you?"

"Not personally, no, but Sadie has been telling me about her forever. She was a lot like Sadie I think— warm, caring, and nurturing."

"Were you ever able to talk to your grandfather?"

"He wasn't the talking type. Once, when I had a crush on a boy, I tried to tell him about it, but Grandpa got so mad I lit out for Sadie's and stayed away for the better part of the day. He had cooled down by the time I got home, but I never tried again. When I got a little older, and I knew he was about to hit me, I would threaten to run off like my mother had. That would calm him down for a while, but there was no reasoning with him."

"How is it that your mother ended up back here to have you?"

"Sadie said my father was a married man who lived in another town. When my mother ran off and took up with him, I don't think she was worried about getting pregnant, just about staying away from my grandfather for the rest of her life. It's funny, isn't it?"

"What is?"

"That the man she was most afraid of was the man she came back to when she found herself alone, hungry, and scared because she was eight months pregnant and not married. If only Grandpa could have been a little more understanding."

"What did he do?"

"He hit her. Knocked her to the floor. Her water gave way just about then, and I was born 15 hours later. Sadie thinks my mother gave up after that. I didn't cry right away, and she was certain I was dead. Sadie tried to tell her otherwise, but she wouldn't listen. She just lay there, fell asleep, and never woke up."

"Who took care of you?"

"Sadie found a wet nurse. I was pretty scrawny, but I

must have something of Grandpa in me, because I survived."

"Where was your grandmother during all of this?"

"She died when Sadie and my mother were just girls."

They were both quiet for a few moments, and then Sean asked one final question. "Do you have *any* good memories of your grandfather?"

"Not many. When I was 12, I remember being thankful that he only hit me. A friend told me that her dad would touch her the way a husband touches a wife."

Sean pulled her very close then and held her securely against his chest. *She's known such awful things, Lord. It's a miracle she's as wonderful as she is.* Sean desperately wanted to tell her that as hard as this life was, it was only temporary and if she chose, she could someday live forever with God, but now did not seem the time to talk of eternal things.

As Charlie cuddled into his side, Sean prayed silently. *Please, Lord, open the door in Your time and use me if it's Your will.*

□ □ □

Sadie had made Charlie a second dress for church, and she wore it that very morning. It was a pale yellow print that brought out the gold color in her hazel eyes. Sean whistled when he saw her in it, and even with their newly discovered love Charlie was so flustered her face turned three shades of red.

They were again having dinner with Duncan and Lora, and this time Charlie was taking a basket of muffins she had baked the day before. Just as they left the house, Charlie stopped Sean with a question. She had copied a word onto a small scrap of paper and, holding it out to him, asked how to pronounce it and what it meant.

"Remission," Sean told her. "Where did you read this?"

Charlie looked uncomfortable. "In your Bible."

"Oh," Sean said simply, as though it didn't matter in the least. "Well, if it's from the verse I'm thinking of, about the shedding of blood, it means forgiveness."

He led the way to the buggy then, his heart pounding in his chest. He kissed Charlie softly as he helped her into the seat, and prayed once again that God would use him to show Charlie that God was the true Forgiver.

□ □ □

"John, the son of Zacharias and Elizabeth, is often referred to as the forerunner of Christ." Pastor Miller had begun his sermon. "We're still studying the life of Jesus Christ, but right now I'd like you to get to know John a little better. We read about John in the books of Matthew and Mark as a man whose 'raiment is made of camel's hair and whose diet is honey and locusts.'

"I think it's important that the Scriptures tell us what John eats and how he dresses so we get a picture of the overall man. They help us to see that John is a man of consistency. But consistent about what? Let's check Mark 1:7. Let me read it to you. 'There cometh one mightier than I after me, the latchet of whose shoes I am not worthy to stoop down and unloose.'

"There isn't a one of us that hasn't heard the phrase, 'He's not good enough to tie my shoes.' This is what John is saying about himself in regard to Jesus Christ. Mark records here that John said he was not worthy even to untie Jesus' shoes.

"What I'm trying to point out to you is that John was a man of great humility and singleness of purpose. He could have sought a life filled with riches, but we see in his food and clothing that he didn't. His purpose was to prepare the way for the Savior, to tell others that the Christ was coming. John knew that nothing was more important than this task.

"John's mission on this earth as the forerunner of Christ was a great one, but he knew he was not *the* Great One. John couldn't save; he pointed the way toward the One who could. John baptized with water, but the One he pointed to would baptize with the Holy Spirit. For salvation we can look only to Christ, as John states in chapter 20, verse 31, 'But these are written, that ye might believe that Jesus is the Christ, the Son of God; and that believing, ye might have life through his name.'"

Charlie could not get Pastor Miller's words out of her mind. He made it sound simple, but it was all so foreign to her. Salvation, the need to be saved, even words and phrases like "forerunner" and "life through His name," were not in her vocabulary.

Charlie had tried to read Sean's Bible in an attempt to please the husband who meant so much to her, but very little of it had made sense. She hoped that as her reading skills improved, more would become clear. Charlie wouldn't have hesitated to ask Sean what something meant in the newspaper, but his Bible was different.

She was afraid to let him know just how limited her knowledge of the Bible was. He said he wasn't going to leave her, but in many ways Sean was just too good to be true, and Charlie was still just a little afraid she would wake up someday and find him gone.

thirty-four

Two weeks later Charlie awoke to discover she was alone in bed. She lay still and tried to calm her frantic heart. She and Sean always got up together. Even when one was awake first, the other lay quietly and waited for the other to waken.

Charlie's mind was racing. It wasn't Sunday, so she knew Sean was not feeding the stock, and the stillness of the house told her he was not fixing breakfast.

Charlie rose from the bed and stood clutching the front of her nightgown, not wanting to face what she had feared from the moment Patrick left town. She walked out to the kitchen on limbs that were stiff with dread, limbs that came alive with action when she spotted the note on the table.

Charlotte,

I've gone to Duncan's. Hartley has been in touch, but he's gone now. I'll be home soon, so stay where you are. Stay out of the livery, and for my peace of mind, don't even answer the door.

Sean

Charlie read the note through twice before running to the bedroom with plans to disobey her husband's every word.

❑ ❑ ❑

"About what time did you hear the noise?" Duncan asked Sean.

"It was just beginning to get light, so I guess around 4:30."

Duncan consulted his pocket watch. "It's been two hours; there's no point in trying to track him now."

"Do you think he's hit the bank?"

"No. I'd have heard by now. You don't seem overly surprised, Sean, that he was able to track you down."

Sean's eyes narrowed in thought for a moment. "I guess it's because I know Hartley so well. I can't say as I've ever felt that Charlotte and I were being watched, but the man has eyes everywhere, if you catch my meaning."

"Connections?"

"Right."

Lora put a plateful of food in front of each man, and Sean was opening his mouth to say he couldn't stay, when all three heard a horse approaching at high speed.

Charlie burst into the kitchen without even knocking, her hand going to her mouth and her eyes closing in relief when she saw that Sean was all right. The young husband rose from the table and took her into his arms. They stood for a few moments in silence, unaware of the older couple watching them, and then Sean led Charlie to the table.

He put her in the chair next to his own and brushed a stray curl from her cheek. He spoke tenderly and without rebuke.

"I know you read the note or you'd have never found me. You also knew I wanted you to stay home and out of the livery."

"Would you have stayed if I'd left you the same note?"

"No," Sean admitted without hesitation, and leaned to press a kiss to her forehead.

Charlie still had hold of Sean's hand when she began to calm down enough to look at the other people in the room. She looked across the table to find Duncan grinning at her.

"Good morning, Charlie."

Charlie couldn't help but smile back. "Hi, Duncan."

A moment later she had her own plate of food, as did Lora, and Duncan was saying grace as though having people interrupt their breakfast was an everyday occurrence.

"Father in heaven, I thank you for this food and for Lora's work; please bless our bodies this day. I would also ask Your guiding hand on our plans concerning Hartley. Protect us, Lord, in Your will, that we might glorify Your name. In Christ's name I pray. Amen."

Charlie ate and listened in silence as the conversation between Sean and Duncan continued. She learned that Sean had heard a noise outside at daybreak. He had gone out dressed in nothing more than his jeans to find Hartley standing by their well.

In the space of a few seconds Hartley told Sean that Rico had been killed in a bank robbery in Los Angeles, and Hartley needed to pull another job because he was out of money. He wanted Sean's help to hit the Visalia bank.

Before Sean could make any reply, the two men heard noises on the street. Hartley left quickly, but told Sean where to meet him on Sunday night, only three days away, so they could make plans.

"He fascinates me, Duncan, because he seemed genuinely shook when he told me about Rico, and then he went on to tell me where I was to meet him, assuming I'd be a part of his gang again."

Duncan shook his head. "He doesn't fascinate Witt. Did you see which way Hartley headed?"

"No, he went around the house."

"But this place where he wants to meet you is only about a 30-minute ride?"

"Right. He didn't give me a time, so I'm going to head out when there's still plenty of light."

"You can't be serious?" Charlie said softly, but no one acknowledged her.

"If he doesn't show, I'll leave him a note and maybe we can still trap him. I still can't believe I went outside without the gun. When Witt finds out he'll be furious."

"You can't be serious?" Charlie's voice, although still an incredulous whisper, was louder this time and heard by everyone. Sean looked at her with great compassion and then explained softly.

"Duncan is not pushing me into this, Charlotte; I volunteered. Hartley would have hit the bank here whether I'd been with him or not, but the truth is, I *was* with him, and now I want to do something to bring him to the law."

Charlie was silent. She stared at Sean as though seeing him for the first time. Without thanking Lora for breakfast or bidding anyone goodbye, she rose from the table and walked out the door. The Duncans and Sean stayed in their places even as they listened to her ride away.

"We'll be praying for you, Sean," Duncan finally said. "And if you change your mind, there will be no hard feelings. I won't talk to Witt until I hear from you."

Sean thanked both husband and wife after those words and went back to the livery to try to reason with his wife.

On their own once again, Lora rose from the table to pour more coffee for Duncan. She would have returned the pot to the stove, but he moved his chair out and patted his knee invitingly. Lora, never needing to be asked twice, sat in her husband's lap. It had been their special way of cuddling since the day they had been married.

"What were you thinking just now as you poured the coffee?"

Lora sighed on the question.

"Don't want to tell me?" he questioned as his arms settled around her waist.

"I guess I don't because it means admitting how faithless I am."

"Charlie," Duncan said in instant understanding. Lora nodded.

"I know all about fears, Lucas, and if she would just turn to God, He would comfort her," Lora said with tender conviction.

"You don't sound very faithless to me."

"My faithlessness comes when I see the complete lack of hope on her young face. She's not the hard person I always believed her to be, but at times she seems so closed to spiritual matters."

"We've got to look at how far she's come already," Duncan told her assuredly. "When you think how quickly they've made their situation livable, it does make you want to see it as the miracle of which Sean talks."

Suddenly Lora hugged him back. "Thank you, Lucas. I needed to hear that."

Still wrapped in one another's embrace, they took a

moment to pray, each thanking God for bringing the Donovans into their world and for whatever purpose He had in doing so.

thirty-five

Charlie had not touched or spoken ten words to her husband since leaving the Duncans. Sean tried to bring her out, but she refused to talk to him.

By Friday night Sean was at the end of his tether. He knew Duncan was waiting for his answer, and even though he wanted to please his wife, this was something he had to do. If only she would talk to him.

Sean pulled the double doors in the front of the livery shut and went to his wife, who was making an expectant mare comfortable for the night.

"Charlotte, can we please talk?" Sean had started the conversation just that way on many occasions, and as before, Charlie ignored him. But Sean had had enough. When Charlie moved away from him he reached for her, but Charlie had second-guessed him and begun to run. A second later she found herself tackled in a stall full of sweet-smelling hay.

She struggled under her husband's weight, but he held her easily. In fact, he simply captured her hands within his own, buried his face in the side of her neck, and waited for her to stop struggling.

It took a little time, but Sean began to feel the tenseness leave her body. The hands he held began to hold him back and Charlie angled her head so that she could kiss her husband's forehead.

"Please don't go," she finally whispered.

"I have to."

"Then let me go with you."

"That's out of the question."

Sean heard her sigh. "Sean, I'm afraid you won't come back alive."

"I know you are," Sean said simply.

Charlie fell silent again. "You're not afraid of death, are you?"

"No. I've settled my eternity with God."

Charlie began to struggle this time so suddenly that Sean let go of her. He watched in surprise as she sprang up and faced him, her hands doubled into fists at her sides.

"I wish someone would tell me what that means!" She was a picture of frustration, and Sean could only gawk as she turned and stormed from the livery.

All this time he had been expecting her to show interest in the things of the Lord, waiting for her to ask questions, when she hadn't even understood what she had been hearing.

Sean would have liked to have taken a few days to pray over this new revelation, but he didn't have time. Charlie was right; he might not come back alive. He had to be certain that Charlie understood before he left. Maybe she wouldn't make a decision, but he had to map it out for her. He would start by apologizing for not explaining in the first place.

◻ ◻ ◻

"Instead of working on your spelling words tonight, Charlotte, I'd rather we talked."

"About Hartley." Charlie's voice was flat.

"No, about something more important than Hartley."

Charlie looked over at Sean from her end of the sofa, only to find him watching her. She couldn't take her eyes off him as he began to share.

"First of all I want to tell you how sorry I am that I haven't explained my faith to you, and how sorry I am that I took for granted you would understand. I'd like to explain now, if you'll let me."

Sean waited for Charlie's nod and then began.

"When I was four I memorized my first two verses from Scripture—John 3:16 and 17: 'For God so loved the world that he gave his only begotten Son, that whosoever believeth in him should not perish, but have everlasting life. For God sent not his Son into the world to condemn the world, but that the world through him might be saved.' I could say the words both frontward and backward but I didn't understand that they applied to me personally until I was six.

"When I was six I began to notice for the first time that my sisters and I looked different from the Hawaiian children with whom we were growing up. I remember asking my mother about it, and she told me it was because we were from a different background. I, of course, wanted to know where all the other people like me were. When she explained, I then wanted to know why we even lived in Hawaii in the first place. When she told me that we were there to tell people about the love of Jesus Christ so they could believe in Him, I told her I'd never prayed and told God I believed in his Son.

"To my surprise she told me she had known that all along, but she never worried because she was certain that as soon as I understood, I would believe, and then I would make that step. She was right. We knelt right there on the sand, and I told God I was a sinner who believed He sent His Son to save me, and Charlotte, that's what I was trying to do with you.

"I was certain that as soon as you heard the words from me or Pastor Miller, you would make a choice for Christ. I lost sight of the fact that I grew up hearing words like 'saved' and 'eternal life,' forgetting that not everyone understands." Charlie was taking in every word, so Sean continued.

"I need to tell you why I believe. First of all, belief is a choice. One of the first acts of faith is believing that the Bible is God's Holy Word, and that the words inside can be trusted and need to be obeyed.

"The Bible tells us that our life on earth is not forever; everyone's physical body dies, but there is life after death. It also says that all men sin and sin separates us from God, but Charlotte, honey, I honestly didn't know how to tell you any of this.

"I've been so afraid that you would think I was saying I'm better than you are, so I held back. I didn't want you to think my love was conditional. Am I making any sense?"

Charlie could only nod, and Sean moved on.

"The Bible teaches that this life on earth is temporary, and following this life is eternity. I know you're not certain that God is there, but I believe with all my heart that He is. And when the time comes for you to die you can either meet God as your Savior, as I will, or you can meet Him as your judge. If you meet Him as your Savior, then you will spend eternity in heaven. If not, then you will spend eternity in hell, separated from God. I have accepted Jesus Christ as my Savior. That's what I meant when I said that my eternity is settled.

"Should I die on Sunday, I know without a doubt that I'll go to be with God. That's why I'm not afraid. I'm not wishing that I'll die, but I'm not afraid either. You can make that choice also, so you don't have to be afraid, Charlie, for yourself or for me."

It was the first time he had called her by her nickname, and it was said so tenderly that it made Charlie tremble.

"Please hold me, Sean," she whispered.

Sean was more than happy to comply. He knew he had given her a lot to think about, and she obviously needed time to take it in. All he could do for the moment was pray that he would be there when she needed him most.

thirty-six

Charlie spent the night wrapped in her husband's arms. Even in sleep she clung to him. In the morning, Saturday, Sean told her he had to meet with Duncan and Witt. Charlie was proud of herself when she didn't argue or cry.

She walked over to Duncan's with him. While the men talked in the kitchen, she stayed in the living room with Lora and tried not to think about the conversation in the other room. She wasn't denying what was to come, but she didn't think she could handle hearing plans that were certain to lead to her husband's death.

❑ ❑ ❑

"I want us to head out around 4:00. Since I'm sure he won't be there until after dark, I've written a note to leave him. I want to play things my way, so the note tells him where we can meet again in a few days."

"I still think we should go after dark," Witt interjected.

"Then tomorrow night would be our only chance, and I don't like those odds," returned Sean. "My way is better. When he finally arrives, he will see tracks made by three horses and know that I'm not coming alone."

Witt was frustrated. "Where is *your* meeting place for Tuesday night?"

"It's only 15 minutes outside of town, but it's far enough away from the bank that he will be lulled into a false sense of security."

Duncan agreed wholeheartedly with Sean's plan, and between the two of them they won Witt over to their way of thinking. The men continued to plan their actions of the next few days with careful precision.

Sean was the first to leave, and Duncan and Witt were able to discuss something that had been on both of their minds. When Witt finally left, Duncan sat down and wrote a letter to the judge who had sentenced Sean to hang.

❑ ❑ ❑

Charlie tried to act normal at Sadie's house on Sunday, and in fact fooled everyone at the dinner table except the man who loved her. Sean could see the strain in her face, and prayed that she would turn to God for comfort.

Sean knew his life on earth held no guarantees, so he didn't dare tell Charlie he would be back. He was confident, however, that they would not see Hartley this day. Still, he said nothing.

In fact, they had barely said a word to each other on any subject when Sean realized it was 20 minutes to 4:00. With a heavy heart he moved toward the livery to saddle Buddy, their best mount. He dreaded leaving Charlie when she was so upset, but he could not for the moment see any help for it.

Charlie stood at the window as Sean tied Buddy's reins to a tree limb and came inside. He wasted no words, but came directly to Charlie and took her in his arms.

"Charlie," he again used her nickname, and she loved the sound on her ears. "If you find you have time on your hands in the next few hours, I want you to do me a favor."

"Lora invited me over."

"I know she did, and I could tell when you thanked her that you didn't plan to go."

"That's true. What did you want me to do?"

Sean reached down to the kitchen table for his Bible. "If you stay here and feel restless, start reading in the book of John." Sean turned to the first chapter and left the Bible open on the table.

"Take down a few notes if something confuses you, and we'll talk about it when I get back."

"Will you be back, Sean?"

"If it's within my power to be here, nothing will keep me away." Charlie thought she would drown in the emotional depths of her husband's eyes.

"I love you," he whispered before his lips covered hers. Charlie clung to him.

When they both heard the approach of other horses, they exited the house together. Sean climbed on his mount and stared down at his wife. He dragged his gaze from hers and stared out in the direction of the meeting place. A second later he leaned from the saddle and pulled Charlie up to his lap. He kissed her long and hard, and then set her back on the ground. This time he didn't look in her direction as he heeled his horse and went with the other men.

❏ ❏ ❏

Charlie paced for 15 minutes before she picked up the Bible and carried the precious Book to her bedroom. She lay down on the bed, snuggled into Sean's pillow, and began to read the first verses.

Charlie made an effort not to get slowed down by unfamiliar words. Reading steadily, she came to John 3:16 and 17 and remembered Sean reciting them to her. Several times her eyes focused over each word before continuing.

Time ceased to exist as she read about Jesus and Nicodemus. Her eyes devoured the story of Jesus and the Samaritan woman, and then on to the sick boy in Capernaum whom Jesus healed, sight unseen.

Chapter after chapter fell away. The feeding of the 5000, Jesus walking on the water, the healing of the blind man, the raising of Lazarus—all became real to her. Page after page revealed Jesus as Shepherd and Lord. With tears pouring down her face, Charlie arrived at the final chapters where God's perfect Son was mocked and crucified for the sins of all men.

By the time Charlie read the last verse in the last chapter, she had cried until her head hurt, and she was wrung dry. She told herself she had to get up and watch for Sean, but before her mind could make her body obey, she fell into an exhausted sleep, with Sean's Bible held in her embrace.

thirty-seven

The men rode out of town with the sun at their backs. There was little talk, and Sean by necessity took the lead. Their pace was steady for about 20 minutes, and then Sean eased off as the terrain became rocky.

Hartley chose his meeting place well; it was secluded from three directions. The hair at the back of Sean's neck stood on end. He knew that Hartley could have them in the sight of his rifle at that very moment. Since he had been the one to betray Hartley, Sean knew he would be the first to die.

But all was quiet. They rode into rocks that resembled a small canyon with no sign of anyone or anything. With plenty of sunlight still available, they completely scouted the area. Had it not been for the fear of Hartley showing up and surprising them, the entire trip would have been anticlimactic.

Sean left his note in a conspicuous place, and the three rode home by way of what was to be the meeting place two nights hence. They didn't tarry and were back in town just at dusk. Witt asked both men to his home in order to go over their plans one more time.

It was well after dark before Sean rode toward home. Seeing from a distance that all was dark, he stopped and checked first with Lora and then with Sadie. He went back home with his heart pounding in his chest. The fear that Charlie might be harmed made his anxiety over Hartley seem a small thing. Without bothering to attend his horse, he tied Buddy outside the house and entered, his heart pleading with God for the safety of his cherished wife.

❑ ❑ ❑

The lantern light flickered over the bedroom walls as Sean's hand trembled. He had come in and called Charlie's name as he lit a lamp, and then after a quick peek into the living room, walked with dread toward the silent bedroom.

Even in the dim light he could make out her puffy eyes and the signs of tears. He set the lantern on the nightstand, turned it high, and eased down beside her. Sean didn't try to remove the Bible from her grasp. He just put his arms around her and kissed her softly on the cheek.

It took a few moments for her to come fully awake and then she only blinked at him, as though she believed herself to be dreaming. One moment she was staring at him, and the next the Bible had fallen to the side and her arms had his neck in a stranglehold. She was sobbing uncontrollably.

"My darling Charlie," Sean crooned softly.

"Are you all right . . . are you really all right?" Charlie gasped through her tears, touching his arms and chest as though checking for injuries.

"I'm fine. We didn't even see Hartley. I just need a bath, since I smell like sweat and horses."

"Sadie won't mind," Charlie hiccuped, thinking they would do anything he wanted, just as long as he was home, safe and sound. "We can go right now."

Sean laughed to himself at her enthusiasm. She had never been easily offended by unpleasant odors before, and he wondered at her nearly frantic state. She grew very quiet on the walk to Sadie's, and Sean told himself he was going to hurry so they could get back home and talk.

ロ ロ ロ

Charlie, still agitated, was trying to scrub the skin off Sean's back when she broke her silence.

"I wanted to wait until we were back home, Sean, but I've got to talk to you."

"All right," he agreed with some relief.

Scooting around the side of the tub, Charlie stayed on her knees and leaned so close to Sean that she soaked the front of her dress. He watched in confusion as fresh tears puddled in her eyes and she began.

"They killed him, Sean—they killed Jesus Christ. He had healed them and fed them and proven to them over and over that He was the Son of God, and they still crucified Him. Why, Sean? If He's really God's Son, He could have saved Himself. Why didn't He?"

Sean's wet hands came up and tenderly cradled her face. His heart was beating so fast he was breathless.

"Because we needed a Savior. Our sin debt to God had to be paid. He loved us enough to be that Savior. Man's sin placed a ravine between God and man, but God in His infinite love bridged that ravine with His own dear Son."

"Oh, Sean." Charlie's tears began in earnest.

Sean's water was quite cold by the time Charlie was done crying and talking about all she had read. She apologized to him several times, but the night was hot and he only smiled. Did she really think a little cold water was important in light of her meeting Jesus Christ? But that wasn't the only question on Sean's mind, and he waited only until they were home in bed before he broached it.

"Charlie, in all your reading, did you understand that you, Charlotte Donovan, must make a decision?"

"You mean the faith and believing you were talking about before?"

"Yes. I don't want to push you; I just want to make sure you understand."

"I do understand, Sean, but I don't think you do. I haven't been a good person and Jesus, well, He's *God's Son*. I don't think He really wanted me—"

"Charlie," Sean called her name softly. "I want you to listen to John 3:16 and 17 again."

"I've read those verses through several times."

"I'm sure you have, but I want you to hear them one more time: 'For God so loved Charlie, that he gave his only begotten Son and if Charlie believes in him, Charlie will not perish, but have everlasting life. For God sent not his Son to condemn Charlie, but that through him, Charlie might be saved.'"

Sean watched her face closely. He saw her struggle, her desire to be loved and accepted, but he stayed quiet and prayed.

"I didn't even believe He existed for a long time."

"That sin and all others were covered on the cross where He was crucified." Again Sean waited and prayed.

"Do you really think He loves me?"

"Absolutely."

Charlie gave a small nod, as though confirming in her mind what she must do. Sean helped her with the words, and in a soft, confident voice she prayed, telling God of her sins and confessing her belief in His Son.

Charlie finally knew peace as she fell yet again into exhausted slumber, this time in her husband's arms. Sean, very mindful of starting Charlie's tears again, held his own until she was asleep.

"I would have waited years, Lord," Sean cried in the dark. "But You've given me another of Your miracles. For this, I thank You."

Sean followed his wife into slumber a few minutes later, but not before he pictured himself and Charlie in the Hawaiian Islands, living and working with the island people he loved so well.

thirty-eight

Charlie's face was puffy in the morning, but the smile she gave her husband when he kissed her awake was beautiful. They were up a little earlier than usual, and Sean answered many questions about the Bible as they readied for work.

Over breakfast the questions continued, and then Sean knew he had to mention Hartley. He prayed that with her newfound faith, Charlie would turn to God with her fears.

"Charlie, I need to tell you some things."

The seriousness in his tone immediately arrested her attention, and even though alarmed, Charlie listened.

"It's true that we didn't see Hartley yesterday, but we did set up another meeting time at a different place."

"How could you have done that?"

"I left him a note."

"When do you meet?"

"Tomorrow night."

"Is Duncan going with you?"

"Not this time; for the plan to be successful both he and Witt are needed here in town."

"You're going out alone?" Charlie's voice was strained.

"Yes. It has to be that way." Sean reached across the table and claimed Charlie's hand. "Would you like me to explain what's going on?"

Sean could see that it took an effort on her part, but she nodded. He explained the situation calmly, and Charlie's mouth dropped open in surprise.

"Whose idea was this?"

"Mine. After working with Hartley, I have a pretty fair idea of the way he thinks." Sean shrugged and then became serious. "Now, long before dark tomorrow night, I'm going to deliver you to Lora's or Sadie's: The choice is yours. But after I take you there you *must not* leave."

"Oh, Sean." Charlie looked as helpless as she felt, but Sean was relentless.

"There will be no discussion on this, Charlie. You can't go with me, and you can't follow me." His look was very stern, and Charlie knew he was right. She would probably get in the way and get them both killed.

"Now, where do you want to go?"

"Lora's," Charlie said with resignation. "She knows more of what's going on, and I know she'll pray with me if I ask her."

Sean's smile was a picture of tenderness. "Speaking of prayer, why don't we ask God right now to protect both of us in the next few days?"

Charlie nodded, and Sean thought his heart would burst as he heard her sweet voice in prayer. She talked to God as she talked to anyone else, only now there was an element of confidence in knowing that she was very loved.

Even though they were now running a little late, husband and wife followed their prayer time with a long embrace before heading out the door for work.

❑ ❑ ❑

If Lora hugged Charlie once she hugged her ten times when she shared the news of how she came to know Jesus Christ. The older woman cried, and just as Charlie expected, Lora was more than happy to pray with her.

Their conversation was animated during the hours they had together. The fact that their husbands might be in danger hung in their minds, but Charlie was full of questions that Lora was happy to answer. They both felt God's presence and His blessing in the time they shared.

❑ ❑ ❑

Sean Donovan was nowhere near as calm as he appeared to be. He had ridden out to the meeting place just as the sun was setting and leaned against a tree as though he had all the time in the world. He was in fact praying until he thought his heart might burst.

"I can hardly believe I'm in this position, Lord. It could have been me. It could have been me they're trapping right now. So many of the choices I've made have been for myself and not You. Thank You, God, for sparing me and giving me another chance.

"Please protect Duncan, Witt, and the others as they put their lives on the line tonight. Please protect them. And Hartley. Oh, God," Sean groaned, "if only I could talk to him about You. I don't know if he would listen, but I'd just like the chance. Help the men to bring him in without harm."

Sean would have prayed on and on if his thoughts had not been interrupted by the sound of approaching hoofbeats. Thinking the entire plan had backfired, he came away from the tree with the rifle cocked and ready. He sagged with relief when he heard Duncan call his name. The older man reined in his horse and sat looking down at Sean in the moonlight.

"It's all over."

"Hartley?"

"In custody."

"So he's alive?"

"He was wounded, shot in the arm, but he's very much alive. It was over so fast I didn't see any point in letting you sit out here much longer."

"Was anyone hurt?"

"Only Hartley. He was alone, and it all happened just like you said it would. He came in the back door, and with his attention riveted on Witt's silhouette in the moonlight at the front of the bank, he never even heard me approach."

"How did he get shot?"

"After he felt my gun at his back he turned and started to draw. His eyes looked a little wild with shock, and I can't say as I blame him. He must have been certain we would all be out here waiting with you."

Sean nodded with resignation. "I want to talk to him."

"I don't see any problem with that, but I think I should warn you—he'll hang, Sean, as sure as I'm sitting here, Hartley will hang."

Sean said nothing to this. He swung himself up into his own saddle and followed Duncan back to town.

❑ ❑ ❑

"I heard you had found God, but I just couldn't believe it." Hartley's mocking voice was like a whip over Sean's back.

The men had been talking for about 20 minutes, and Sean could see that Hartley still believed himself invincible. Any attempt Sean made to discuss God or eternity was met with open contempt. He couldn't really blame him, but it hurt. Unfortunately, that wasn't the worst of it.

"You're completely unrepentant," Sean commented to the older man, his voice soft with pain.

"Now you sound like a preacher," Hartley sneered through the bars, and turned away.

Sean could see the conversation was over. He was turning away himself, but before Sean could leave Hartley made it clear that he didn't want to see him again. Sean really couldn't blame him, but it hurt more than he could have imagined.

❑ ❑ ❑

"He was a bank robber before the two of you ever met, Sean. Try to keep that in mind." Lora's words and gentle manner were like a balm applied to an open wound. "*You* did not make him choose the life he did, and even today when he had a chance to discuss eternal things, he again made his choice."

Sean thanked her softly and held his wife's hand a little tighter. Sean had turned down refreshments in the Duncans' living room, needing for the moment only to sit and be ministered to emotionally.

"When is the trial, Duncan?" Charlie wanted to know.

"Tom should be here by Thursday, so the proceedings should be no later than Friday afternoon."

There was little conversation after that, and finally, a little before midnight, Sean and Charlie both received hugs from Lora and went home. They stopped outside the front doors of the livery long enough to post a note, stating that they wouldn't be open before noon. It was wise planning since they both slept until 11:00 A.M.

thirty-nine

Sean seemed preoccupied for the next two days. He and Charlie prayed together at every meal and then before bed, but his heart was so burdened for Hartley (and how clearly he remembered being in the jail cell himself) that he was a bit quiet and withdrawn.

Charlie didn't know what to say or do for her husband, so she too was quiet. Quite unexpectedly, Kaitlin came to the rescue by sending a box just for Charlie.

"Lunch is here, Sean," Charlie called to her spouse, who went immediately to wash up for the meal. They had thanked God for the food and begun to eat when Pete's son, from the general store, arrived with the box.

"My dad asked me to bring this over. It's for you, Charlie, from Santa Rosa."

Charlie didn't do anything more than look at the box, even when the boy placed it at her feet and went on his way. She glanced at it several times, and then felt her husband's eyes on her.

"Aren't you going to see what it is?"

"I think I'll wait until after lunch."

Sean was a bit surprised that she wasn't more curious, and for the first time since Hartley had been caught he realized how little conversation they'd had in the last two days.

He was on the verge of telling her his feelings when they were interrupted by a customer who wanted his horse shod. The afternoon gave no time for anything save hard work. Again, conversation between man and wife was delayed.

At closing time, Charlie went to the house to set the table for supper, and Sean closed up the livery. He took one final look around before heading toward the door, and that's when he spotted Charlie's box. He tucked it under one arm and went to have his meal.

The box wasn't mentioned until after the supper dishes had been washed and dried. It had been Sean's night to wash, and Charlie, thinking he had finished up and gone into the living room, turned away from hanging her drying towel to find he was sitting back at the kitchen table, the box next to him, watching her.

She looked decidedly uncomfortable, and Sean's mind raced to figure out why. And as Charlie had done so many times past, she put Sean's questions to rest with the first sentence out of her mouth.

"Why do you suppose your sister sent me a box and not you, her own brother?"

"Well," Sean thought a moment. "She already sent me one, and there's nothing else I really need." He smiled encouragingly and pushed the box in her direction.

Charlie looked unconvinced. She touched it tentatively and then with a quick look at Sean, opened the top.

"Oh, my," Charlie breathed as she held up very feminine linen undergarments and bed attire. There were two shifts, a camisole, a nightgown, and a pair of bloomers. Charlie stood fingering all of them for some minutes before she remembered Sean.

"Oh," she said in dismay as she held the nightgown in her arms. "There's nothing for you. I really thought there would be."

Sean's eyes twinkled as one dark eyebrow lifted. "On the contrary, I think everything in there is for me." He laughed softly and pulled Charlie into his lap when she blushed to the roots of her hair.

"Why didn't you want to open the box?" he asked as Charlie leaned against his chest.

Charlie sighed. "The past few days have been so hard for you, and I wanted to do something to make them easier. Instead, all I've done is sit back and watch you. Then this box arrived not addressed to you, and I thought that might make you feel even worse."

"I love your honesty," he told her simply. "And it's my own fault that the last few days have been hard. I've been picturing myself in Hartley's shoes, and believe me, it's easy to do when you've been there. But that's not the worst of it. I've been so worried about Hartley's future that I've forgotten the here and now."

"The here and now?"

"You, Charlie. You are the here and now. I can't do anything for Hartley. The judge will determine his fate, and unless Hartley asks to see me, I won't talk to him again before he hangs or goes to jail for the rest of his life. There is nothing I can do about that. But my darling wife, who happens to be a new believer in Christ and needs much nurturing and guiding, well, let's just say I can see now that I've been neglecting her. I'm sorry."

Charlie kissed him and told him she didn't feel at all neglected. Sean wasn't convinced, but the door was opened for a full evening of sharing. Sean told Charlie everything he was feeling, and Charlie, who had been holding off with more questions about God, was able to question Sean to her heart's content.

It was past the time they both should have been asleep when Charlie ended the night with one more question.

"Sean," she said in a sleepy voice, "why do you call me Charlie now and not Charlotte?"

He answered after a moment. "Charlie was too familiar when we were first married, and then after getting to know you, I wanted you to understand that I look at you as a man does a woman. The name Charlie wasn't very fitting in that case. But suddenly you just became my darling Charlie, and I rarely even think of calling you Charlotte anymore. Which name do you prefer?"

"Charlie," the sleepy redhead answered with a tired sigh. "Or my darling Charlie. Either one will do."

forty

Duncan's prediction for the trial proceedings proved to be very accurate. At 1:30 on Friday afternoon the courthouse was jammed with people, and Judge Harrison was up front trying to silence the crowd.

Sean, on hand because both Duncan and Witt told him he might be needed, found that if given a choice, he would not have been present. His own trial came back to haunt him. The chairs in the room, the fear he felt, the very smell of the place were all too evocative, and Sean felt himself break out into a cold sweat. He repeatedly thanked God for sparing him until he was once again able to breathe normally.

Charlie had decided not to come, even though both Lora and Sadie were in the courtroom. It did Sean's heart good to know that she was waiting for him at the livery.

As it was, Sean's testimony was not needed. Witt had done his homework well, and the evidence stacked against Hartley was more than enough to convict him. Surprisingly, Sean felt nothing but a calm acceptance when he heard the judge announce that Hartley would hang on the following day.

Sean was one of the first out of the courtroom, but he had only been back at the livery for some 20 minutes when Duncan showed up. He was more than willing to accompany the sheriff back to the jail when Duncan said Hartley wished to see him.

Another 20 minutes passed before Sean exited the jail once again, heavy of heart. He had been so certain that Hartley had wanted to discuss his eternity. Instead, all he had wanted from Sean was help breaking out of jail. Sean had stared at him incredulously, but Hartley had been very serious. All talk of anything else was rejected, and Sean went on his way.

Charlie had only to look at her husband to know it had not gone well. She put her arms around his waist. They stood inside the door of the forge without speaking. Charlie knew Sean would share when he was ready.

"I prayed for you," she whispered.

"Thank you, darling."

It wasn't the first time Charlie had said such a thing to him, but it never failed to give him a tight sensation in his chest. She was so precious, and knowing they were going to spend eternity together only heightened the love in his heart.

Before Sean went back to work he took a moment to remind himself of his own words to Charlie concerning Hartley.

"You've taken it out of my hands, Lord. Please help me to leave it with You."

Thankfully, Sean knew peace in his surrender, even though he felt pain over the loss. Hartley was executed the next afternoon. The date was July 1, 1876.

forty-one

Sean felt it was very odd to have a hanging in town on the first of July and a celebration on the fourth, but that was just what Visalia had.

Nearly all businesses were closed on this special centennial day, and the livery was no exception. It felt just like Sunday to the Donovans, and they took advantage of the time to lounge in bed and talk. For the first time in days the conversation was not about Hartley.

"I love the letter your sister included with the clothes she sent. I'm going to write back to her this week."

"I should have known why Kate wanted to know your size."

"She asked you about my size?" Charlie was surprised.

"That she did. Both she and Marcail have a weakness for frilly underclothes, and I think they figure all women do."

"You must have told her the terrible shape all my clothes are in."

"Charlie!" Sean was shocked. "I would never tell my sister such a personal thing."

"I guess you wouldn't." She sounded apologetic.

"But while we're on the subject," Sean went on, "why don't you buy some more new underthings? You're always picking up new things for me, but neglecting your own wardrobe."

"I just don't care to shop for myself, and I don't have an eye for just the right thing like Sadie does. Do you hate my things an awful lot?"

"I don't hate them at all, but everything has holes in it. It's not as if business is slow and we can't afford it."

"That's true. Does your sister order her things through the mail?"

"No. Rigg carries everything imaginable for the mercantile, and Katie and Marcail usually have their pick." Sean's voice had softened, and Charlie became very attentive.

"You miss them, don't you?"

"More than I can say," he admitted. "Kate usually organized a picnic on the Fourth of July, and then of course there were always fireworks."

"I know it won't be the same, but we'll have fireworks tonight. Everyone says they're to be spectacular, since it's the centennial celebration!" Charlie spoke enthusiastically, trying to erase the lonely look from her husband's face.

Sean was quiet, and Charlie rolled on her pillow so she could better see his face. He appeared resigned to the situation, but she could see the sorrow in his eyes. It took a moment for Sean to realize he was under her scrutiny, but Charlie spoke before he could question her.

"Five years is a long time, isn't it?"

"Yes, it is, but in light of never seeing them again, it's no time at all."

"If you could leave town, Sean, I would try to get someone to take the livery."

"Thank you, darling," Sean said simply, reaching to hold her and thinking the subject was settled. But Charlie had more on her mind.

"Sean, if you didn't have to be here for five years, would you want us to move away?" Charlie didn't know why she asked; she just needed to know.

The white-sand beaches of Hawaii immediately swam before Sean's eyes as he answered. "I want us to live wherever God wants us to live. Since I'm bound here for five years, I don't even need to ask God about moving right now. After that time, if we feel led to move on, I'm confident that God will show us where and when."

"I think I knew you would say that, but what I want to know is, where? Where would you like to move if you could?"

"Well, I've thought about Santa Rosa and even San Francisco, but Hawaii was home for so long, I guess my mind always goes there first."

"Would I like Hawaii?"

The question so surprised Sean that he raised up on one elbow to look down at her.

"Why did you ask me that?"

"I don't know. It's just that since I've been married to you, I'm a little restless, and even though you're a great smithy, you always look just a little out of place working in the forge."

Sean couldn't believe what he was hearing. "You mean you would be willing to give up the livery and move away from Sadie?"

Charlie thought for a moment and said yes, but she knew it was safe to do so because they wouldn't have to make a decision for nearly five years.

The subject was dropped then, but Sean was very pleased. *It's a long time in the future*, he thought, *but it sure feels good to know that Charlie is receptive to the idea of moving.*

It never once occurred to him that she was agreeable partly because the possibility was years away.

❑ ❑ ❑

Sean and Charlie went for a midmorning breakfast over at Sadie's. They prayed together before they left the house since Sean knew that Charlie was waiting excitedly for a time when she could share with Sadie what had happened in her life. But Charlie told him she knew how busy Sadie was going to be on this day and was certain there would be no opportunity.

The town's festivities began at noon with a huge potluck lunch. Sean and Charlie sat with Lucas and Lora Duncan, and as always, Sean felt the mix of emotions from townspeople. He was greeted with both smiles and glares, something he had learned to take in stride.

It would have surprised most of the people to know that he understood completely. Not many knew of the part he played in Hartley's arrest, and wanting to be accepted for himself, Sean preferred it that way. But Duncan had been at work, and all of this changed when Judge Harrison, who had been asked to speak at the centennial ceremonies, was closing his speech.

"It's a scorcher out here today, so I won't keep you much longer, but recently something has been brought to my attention, and I've acted upon it. I feel now is the best time to share it with you.

"When I was called here in April, I judged a young stranger who had helped rob your bank. Well, most of you know that through fortuitous circumstances, one of your own townswomen came forward and married that young man, thereby rescuing him from the hangman's noose. This was done within the bounds of the law and it still stands, but I've amended the document I read to you back in April.

"Patrick Sean Donovan III, 'Sean' to most of you, is now a free man. The clause in the aforementioned document, stating that he must live in and serve the community of Visalia for no less than five years, is now amended.

"In case any of you feel outrage at this change, I will tell you this." Judge Harrison's voice rose with intensity. "It was Sean Donovan's plan and his willingness to risk personal injury that brought Hartley to the law this week past. Hartley, a man who has long plagued your town, is dead and will torment you no more because of the efforts of Sheriff Lucas Duncan, Franklin Witt, and Sean Donovan."

The judge said no more, but the applause was thunderous as he exited the platform. Most of the people had stood, but Sean and Charlie sat still in their seats, feeling nothing but shock.

They finally stood and Sean reached for Charlie's hand. A moment later they were surrounded by people. There were still many who hung back, but most of the townsfolk came up to thank or congratulate their local outlaw-turned-hero. Even when the throng pressed close, Sean never once let go of Charlie's hand, so he knew the exact instant she collapsed.

forty-two

It's incredibly hot out there, Sean. I'm surprised more people haven't fainted."

"But you're not certain it's just the heat?"

"No, I can't really tell you anything else until I talk with Charlie."

"Sean?" Charlie called to him in a confused voice.

The frightened young husband turned swiftly at the sound of his wife's voice. They were at the doctor's house, and Charlie was stretched out on the sofa in the dining room that had been converted into an office. Sean quickly knelt by her and cradled her pale cheek with his hand.

"Hi." He spoke the small word, unsure if he should say more. Charlie's complexion was ashen, and she looked completely disoriented.

"Sean," her voice was desperate now, "I'm going to be sick."

The doctor stepped in, and Sean felt every bit of his wife's pain as she vomited into a basin. When she was done, Sean was equally pale.

Charlie wanted to sit up after the doctor mopped her face with a cool cloth. When she did, Sean sat next to her.

She leaned her head against his shoulder, and the doctor pulled a chair close to question her.

"Was it the heat, Charlie, or something more?"

"I don't know, Doc. I did feel pretty warm, but there was no warning. Suddenly everything started to get fuzzy and then black. My head hurts now."

"I can probably give you something for that, but first I need to ask a few questions."

Charlie was questioned about whether or not the heat had ever bothered her before, her diet, sleeping habits, alcohol intake, everything. Charlie answered all questions with calm patience, until the last one.

"Is there a chance you're in a family way?"

Charlie blinked at the man across from her, and then turned to look at Sean. They had talked of children, but neither one had given much thought to the fact that Charlie could be expecting.

The doctor took in the comical looks on the young couple's faces, and had to stop himself from shaking his head. To what did they think the intimate side of marriage led?

"I take it there is a possibility?" the doctor questioned dryly. When Charlie nodded he became much more specific. His questions made her eyes go wide, not because she was offended, but because he was able to tell her exactly what had been happening in her body of late. Nothing very noticeable, but distinct nevertheless.

"I thought women got sick when they were pregnant," Charlie commented. "I'm eating like I always have."

"No, you're not," Sean cut in. "You haven't wanted any coffee in the morning for a couple of weeks, and you're taking in more food than I've ever seen you eat."

Sean left them alone while the doctor examined Charlie, who told her as he finished that she was going to have a child in about seven months. He advised her to go home for the rest of the day, and even though she didn't want to miss any of the festivities, she complied after Sean promised to let her attend the fireworks that night.

Duncan, Lora, Sadie, and most surprisingly, Witt, were all waiting for the Donovans outside. Upon hearing the young couple's news, hands were shook and hugs were given before Sean ushered his wife home and into bed.

❑ ❑ ❑

Charlie slept for two hours, and Sean sat in the living room and prayed. He marveled at how swiftly things had changed from this morning's conversation to Judge Harrison's announcement.

He wondered how Charlie felt about it. He knew she desperately wanted to please him, but if they were supposed to go to Hawaii or even Santa Rosa, it had to be because *both* of them knew they were to move from their present home.

The idea of leaving Duncan and Lora was painful, but the thought of seeing Kate, Marcail, and the family, or possibly living near them or Father was so exciting it took his breath away.

Sean prayed for calm. The change in the document did not make every dream come true. Charlie was his wife, his most precious possession, and if she wanted to stay in Visalia, they would stay. Sean decided right then and there not to mention it to her. He would give her time, and when she was ready, she would talk to him.

For an instant Sean's mind had completely forgotten the baby. As he remembered, he suddenly found himself smiling at absolutely nothing. His darling Charlie was going to have a baby. He once again bowed his head in prayer, this time in praise to God for the miracle in his wife's womb.

❏ ❏ ❏

Lying on her back, Charlie woke slowly and without moving. She frowned at the ceiling for a moment, trying to figure out why she was in bed. When she remembered, her hand slid to her still-flat abdomen. She was going to have Sean's baby.

A smile of pure contentment crossed her face. She had fallen asleep dreaming of a little boy with his father's black hair and eyes. Charlie was still praying, thanking God for the baby and praying for a safe arrival, when Sean came quietly into the room.

"Hi," he whispered. She grinned at him.

He lowered himself to the edge of the bed and bent to kiss her. When Sean sat back there were tears in her eyes.

"Anything I can do?" he asked gently, and Charlie bit her bottom lip as a single tear spilled down her temple.

"There's just been so much, Sean, so much. I never dreamed there could be so many changes, but in the months since we've been married, my life has been completely altered. I mean, they're good changes, but sometimes I'm a little overwhelmed. Like right now."

Charlie couldn't go on, and Sean leaned over to put his arms around her. She had summed it all up rather nicely. They were good changes, but they were a little overwhelming.

They talked about the baby for a long time, and then had a light supper before joining Duncan and Lora, this time to watch the fireworks display. All agreed it was a perfect end to a wonderful day.

forty-three

Charlie's twenty-fourth birthday was five days away when Sean went to the general store hoping to find her a present. The attitudes of the townspeople had changed toward Sean, and even though he had never felt threatened, he was surprised over how many smiles now came his way. Sean was not at all offended by the changes. He only hoped that with the new acceptance he would have opportunities to share about the One who had changed him.

Pete, the owner of the general store, sported an attitude which was remarkably different than in his first encounter with Sean. He greeted the younger man warmly when he walked through the door.

"Hello, Sean. You must be here about Charlie's birthday."

Sean's mouth dropped open in surprise, and the older man chuckled. "Sadie was just in," he said by way of explanation. Sean smiled in return.

"What did she buy?"

"Fabric. I would guess for a skirt or something."

Sean nodded and began to look around. He lingered over the fabric himself, but he wouldn't have known what to ask Sadie to make. The tools distracted him for a time, but then he got down to business. He studied the writing supplies for a long time, and after picking out what he thought to be perfect, a lone book on the shelf caught his eye.

He picked it up and checked the spine. He nearly did a double take when he read the words *Holy Bible*. Sean emptied his hands of all else and inspected the fat volume. He could hardly believe what he was seeing. The top was dusty, but the book itself appeared to be brand-new. He carried it over to Pete.

"Pete, is this Bible for sale?"

"Yeah, although I've had it for years. Some woman ordered it, but she never came back to collect, so it's just been sitting here all this time."

"How much do you want for it?"

The price Pete named was more than reasonable, and, intending to purchase it, Sean set the Bible down on the counter. His hands had gone to the pocket of his jeans when he spotted a small case of jewelry with a glass top. His eyes caressed the 14K gold wedding bands, ranging in price from $1.19 to $4.79. His look was tormented when he glanced back at the Bible.

"Why don't you give her both?" Pete spoke softly.

Sean's hand went again to his pants pocket, and he dug out the money he had brought along.

"If you don't have it now, you can bring it to me later. I won't even put it on the bill."

Sean hesitated for only a moment. "Thanks, Pete," he said gratefully, and in a few minutes was back on the street, the Bible wrapped in plain brown paper and the simple gold band tucked safely in his pocket.

❑ ❑ ❑

Charlie's birthday was on a Sunday, and her first surprise of the day was breakfast in bed. As Sean set the tray down, he looked so satisfied with himself that Charlie couldn't help but laugh.

"You're looking very pleased with yourself." She spoke as she shook out her napkin, and then started as something fell from it and hit the tray. Charlie stared at the small gold band that had landed near her coffee cup and then at her husband.

His smile was shy, and Charlie's heart melted. She didn't talk but picked up the ring, gave it to her husband, and presented her left hand. Sean gladly did the honors, and Charlie's eyes shone as the smooth gold band slid onto the third finger of her left hand.

"Happy Birthday, my darling," Sean whispered when the band was firmly in place, and Charlie leaned close to kiss him.

The breakfast was more than Charlie alone could handle, so she and Sean sat together on the bed and shared from the tray. As was the norm these last days, they talked of the baby, which Charlie had figured was due in early February. But as was also the norm these days, Sean sensed that something was bothering his dear wife.

Knowing she was genuinely excited about the baby, he couldn't help but wonder what was troubling her. Though she never mentioned it, he speculated often as to whether or not she was thinking about what Judge Harrison had said on the Fourth of July. Sean prayed every day about God's purpose in such a pardon. He believed with all his heart that God would lead them in His time, so he felt it best not to press her.

Sadie had asked them to a special dinner that afternoon, so they headed in the direction of the boardinghouse as soon as church was dismissed. To Charlie's delight, Sadie had also asked Duncan and Lora.

The meal was a great success, and Charlie was surprised again when both Lora and Sean handed her packages. She had already opened a package from Sadie containing a skirt and blouse, and of course her ring from Sean.

The five of them were crowded into Sadie's private parlor. Lora and Duncan exchanged a glance as Charlie peeled back the wrapping paper on the hard, flat gift.

"Oh, my," Charlie said in disbelief as she held up a beautiful daguerreotype of the livery. "Where did you get this?"

Duncan smiled at how pleased she looked. "One of the photographers who wandered around town the week of the Fourth was in and tried to sell me a picture of my office. When I spotted the one he'd done of the livery, he told me he was headed to see you. I couldn't resist buying it myself."

Charlie passed the picture to Sean, and his face split with a grin. He knew in an instant that it had been taken the day before the Fourth because he remembered seeing the photographer setting up and wondering what he wanted. Sean was smack in the middle of the picture, framed by the double doors and reaching toward his back pocket for his handkerchief.

Framed in beautifully etched wood, the photo was examined by each and every one. Charlie thanked both Duncan and Lora, and Sean asked her to open the last gift. Charlie threw him a suspicious look before giving her attention to the gift he had placed in her lap. The whole room erupted with laughter at the way she babbled after the gift was unwrapped.

"Oh, Sean; oh, my! My very own Bible! I can't believe it! Do you know how badly I've wanted one? Where did you find this? Oh, look at the pages! Isn't it beautiful? I can't believe it—my very own Bible!"

Charlie moved to her husband's chair and threw her arms around his neck. He laughed as she tried to squeeze the life from him. She thanked him repeatedly and had to stop herself from sitting down to read it right on the spot.

Sadie went to ready the cake and coffee after the presents were put aside. Charlie joined her in the kitchen, giving the younger woman a chance to mention her Bible.

"You must wonder how I could be so excited about receiving a Bible," Charlie began tentatively.

"It has crossed my mind that there's been a change in you," Sadie said matter-of-factly.

"I'd like to tell you about it sometime, Sadie."

The older woman turned her full attention to her niece. She studied the fervent young face for a moment and tried to put her finger on the change. At first she had attributed it to having a happy marriage with a handsome husband and a baby on the way, but Sadie could see there was more.

"This means a lot to you, doesn't it?" Sadie asked quietly.

"Yes, it does."

Sadie suddenly smiled. "Well, honey, if it means that much to you, I'll listen to all you have to say."

They were not given any further time for talk, but Charlie praised God for opening a door. Even as the cake was served by Sadie's capable hands, Charlie prayed about the future opportunity she would have to speak with her aunt.

When Sean and Charlie did head home, Charlie immediately sat down to read her Bible. She had read Sean's on many occasions, but this was somehow special. As always, Charlie prayed that God would show her just what He would have her to see as she read the words, but she never dreamed of the things she would discover in the weeks to come.

forty-four

In other words, we should never have been married?" Charlie was looking very distressed, and Sean searched for some way to explain something he didn't fully understand himself. They were studying in 2 Corinthians, the sixth chapter.

Sean began carefully. "People who have made a decision for Jesus Christ are commanded not to marry someone who does not share that belief, and I was no exception. But everything happened so fast. I want to say that I had no choice in the matter, that I probably could have spoken up and stopped everything, but the truth is, such a thing never occurred to me.

"I had come to a complete peace about dying, even though I was scared of the way that rope would feel. When Duncan removed the noose, I was in a state of shock. Less than ten minutes later, we were husband and wife."

Sean paused before continuing. He wanted Charlie to understand that God never condones sin, but that God's sovereign will is always in play. "Darling," Sean went on gently, "believing that God has complete command of life and death, I have to assume He sent you to keep me on this earth for a while longer. Had we met under normal circumstances, it would have been wrong of me to even court you."

Charlie looked at Sean for a moment and then down at her Bible to read verses 14 through 16 again: "Be ye not unequally yoked together with unbelievers; for what fellowship hath righteousness with unrighteousness? And what communion hath light with darkness? And what concord hath Christ with Belial? Or what part hath he that believeth with an infidel? And what agreement hath the temple of God with idols? For ye are the temple of the living God; as God hath said, 'I will dwell in them, and walk in them; and I will be their God, and they shall be my people.'"

"Who is Belial?" Charlie asked softly.

"That's one of the many names for Satan."

Charlie nodded. "I rather figured you would say that, considering everything else written here."

"Charlie, tell me what you're thinking."

The confused redhead gave a small shrug. "It's just hard to think of our marriage as a sin." Charlie held her hand up when Sean began to protest.

"What if I hadn't come to Christ?"

"I've thought about that. First of all, I know my love for you would never change. Second, I've confessed the sins of the past and known God's forgiveness and fellowship. Nevertheless, there have been numerous consequences from those sinful years. I've hurt people I love dearly, and all I can come up with is, God *did* spare my life, so I would have tried to serve Him as best I could, even with an unsaved wife."

Charlie gave a small sigh and looked again at the Bible in her lap. "There's so much to learn, isn't there?"

"Yes there is, but God is infinitely patient." Sean reached for her hand. "He knows our hearts and understands each and every struggle."

Charlie didn't answer because she didn't want Sean to know what she was *really* struggling with. Finding out what the Bible taught about marriage between believers and unbelievers was a little upsetting. But after some thought Charlie could see how much sense it made.

On the other hand, her real struggle was much harder to define. It was a mix of knowing how right Sean looked with a Bible in his hand, and less so with a hammer, and also knowing that if they so chose, they could leave Visalia whenever they wanted. Charlie was well aware of the fact that Sean, after all these weeks, had never mentioned the surprising announcement made on Independence Day. This told her one thing—he was waiting for her to bring it up. But as much as Charlie wanted to talk about it, she was scared. It would be some weeks before she understood that God was waiting to take care of that fear.

❑ ❑ ❑

Charlie, now six months along in her pregnancy, stood rubbing her back. The dishes were put away, and Sean had already retired to the living room to read the paper. With her free hand, Charlie felt the very distinct swelling in the front of her skirt. She was not very big, but the baby moved constantly, telling her there was indeed a little person growing inside.

Charlie looked at the doorway of the living room and still she hesitated. It was time to talk with Sean. She was still a little afraid of the future, but it was time to bring her fears to her husband. God had shown her many places in Scripture that assured her of His love and control, and Charlie found comfort in these verses. But God had also given her a husband, a man who loved God and wanted His will. It was time she talked to him about those fears.

Sean smiled as Charlie took a place on the couch beside him. Reaching for her hand, Sean studied her face in the lantern light. The pregnancy was making her tired, but she was far and away the most beautiful woman in the world to him.

Quite often when they sat together in the evening, Sean would lean over her swollen tummy and talk to their baby. But tonight he perceived that Charlie needed all of his attention.

"Anything I can do?" It was Sean's standard line when he sensed that Charlie needed to talk, and as he had hoped, it did the trick.

"*I'm* being a baby," Charlie admitted softly.

"About what?"

"About our moving away."

Sean didn't reply to this, and after a silent moment Charlie continued.

"You're a good blacksmith, Sean, one of the best I've seen, and I've seen a few. But something hasn't been right from the very beginning, and it took my coming to Christ to understand what that *something* is. You look better with a Bible in your hand.

"I don't know if that makes any sense, but I just can't see you pounding on horseshoes for the rest of your life. It's taken me awhile, but just after you said that you always think of Hawaii when you dream of us living elsewhere, Judge Harrison publicly pardoned you. I just knew that someday God would direct us away from here, and the truth is I'm scared to death."

Sean reached for Charlie and pulled her into his arms. "And you thought," he finished gently, "that the second

I knew you were willing to move, I would make you pack and drag you out of town."

"Something like that," Charlie admitted softly.

"Well, it's not going to happen that way, darling, because I don't know if we're supposed to go anywhere. I picture us working as missionaries, just as my folks did, but I don't know where, and God might have Visalia in mind for another 20 years."

"And you could be happy, Sean?"

"Definitely. Now I have a question for you. Could you be happy if God shows us in an unmistakable way that we're to move from here?"

Charlie was silent for only a moment. "You know, for the first time in my life I think I could. Some of the fear is still there, because everything beyond this town is unknown territory to me, but if you're beside me and we know we're headed where God wants us to go, I'll be fine."

Sean watched the front of Charlie's skirt lift with the baby's movement. His hand when to her abdomen as it often did to feel the baby move within her. No words were necessary for a time.

"Do you still wish we could serve the Lord in Hawaii?" Charlie asked.

"Yes, but not before spending some time with my family in Santa Rosa. It's been far too long since I've seen them."

"We could go for a visit, you know."

"That's true. Maybe after the baby is born."

"Let's plan on it."

"All right. Who will run the livery?" Sean wanted to know.

"I don't know, but if we're supposed to go for a visit, then God will send just the person we need."

Sean hugged her again. She'd grown so much in the last weeks, and he couldn't begin to tell her what an encouragement she was. He ended their evening by calling her his darling Charlie and telling her she was the love of his life.

forty-five

Two weeks had passed since Sean and Charlie had talked about moving. The conversation had opened new doors between them, and they were now able to pray and discuss all possibilities with ease. But the real test of faith was upon them, and it was delivered in the form of their new friend, Franklin Witt.

All Charlie had ever heard about Visalia's banker had been put to rest as she got to know the man better. He had become something of a champion to the young Donovans, even before the judge's surprising announcement. He never failed to inquire over Charlie's health with real concern, and it was not at all unusual to see him lounging in the livery, sharing friendly conversation.

Never before had he come on business, but this particular morning things were about to change. The morning had flown by, and the livery owners were just finishing lunch. Sean, always very concerned about Charlie overdoing, had almost convinced her to go to the house and lie down.

"I can take care of everything here," Sean urged.

"Mrs. Franks' mare doesn't like you, and she still needs shoes."

"I'll leave her for last so you'll still have plenty of time to take a nap before coming to help me."

"I'm not tired," Charlie replied stubbornly.

Sean shook his head. She was exhausted. Charlie had not slept well, but she wouldn't hear of it when Sean tried to convince her to stay in bed that morning. He could see that he was going to have to become very stern.

"I want you to go to bed, Charlotte, and I mean now."

Charlie frowned at his tone and the order, but Sean leveled her with a look that told her he meant business. She turned ungraciously for the back door just as Witt came in the front.

"I'm glad I caught you together. Have you got a minute? There's something I need to tell you."

"Actually Charlie was just headed to the—"

"Now is fine, Witt," Charlie interrupted, ignoring the look Sean gave her.

"Well, I just had a man come into the bank who wants to set up a livery in this town. He told me he'd rather buy this one, but didn't really think it would be for sale. Either way, he plans to borrow money to open a livery."

"What's his name?" Sean asked suspiciously, and Witt answered, "Zach Carlton."

Husband and wife exchanged a glance. A man named Zach Carlton had been in just two days ago to rent a horse. He had been far from casual about his interest in every square inch of Cooper's Livery. Sean had tried to question him about whether he had business in town or was just passing through, but he'd been very evasive.

"I can see that I've surprised you, and I don't expect you've ever given it any thought, so why don't I come by tomorrow and you can tell me if you're at all interested?" The Donovans agreed and thanked Witt for his trouble before he went on his way.

"We definitely need to talk about this," Sean quietly told his now-pale wife, "but not until after you've slept."

This time Charlie did not argue, and after Sean put out the sign saying he would be back in 15 minutes, he escorted his wife to the house. He stayed with her until she was asleep, which took less than five minutes, but it was far more than five minutes before Sean was done praying and able to concentrate on his work.

❑ ❑ ❑

Sean had been desperate for a bath that night, so husband and wife decided that when they returned from Sadie's they would go to bed early to talk about Witt's news. Neither one had taken the time to open the mail, so when they were finally snuggled in bed, Charlie started with the letter from Aunt Maureen, and Sean read a letter from Katie. Kate's letter ended with news about Father.

"Don't be concerned if you don't hear from Father for some time. He wrote that he was so busy with the work there, he didn't know which way was up. He said that God is moving in mighty ways throughout the villages. He also asked us to pray with him that God would burden other families to come and join the work there, and of course for the furtherance of the gospel of Christ."

When it was time to trade, Sean hesitated. Charlie looked at him with some surprise.

"Bad news?"

"No, but Katie reports something Father said, and I really want us to talk before you read it."

Charlie looked at Sean for the space of a few heart-beats, her brows raised in surprise. Sean suddenly realized he was selling her short and handed her the letter. His desire not to pressure her about moving wasn't even valid. She could just as easily have been the first to read Kate's letter and know what Father had said.

Sean also realized it was unfair of him to believe that God would pressure them at all. He was, most likely, giving them some direction. A few minutes later the letters were put aside and Charlie used that very word.

"This is what I've prayed for, Sean," Charlie began. "This is exactly what I've prayed for."

"What is that exactly?"

"Direction. I've prayed that God would show us what direction He wanted us to go and in a way that we could never doubt. I think we know that now."

Sean was speechless and for some reason, fearful. "Charlie, when we were first married, I could tell that you wanted desperately to please me. And now I'm just a little afraid that you're doing it again and—"

"I'm not," Charlie said with a smile. "I mean, pleasing you is important to me, and you don't fear moving because you've been where we're probably headed, but none of what I've said stems from any desire other than to follow God's will."

Sean's heart overflowed with praise to God. He realized then that his wildest dreams were coming true. Charlie saw the emotion in his face and moved close to hold him.

"Oh, Charlie," Sean's voice was breathless, "I thought my life was over, and then you came forward and rescued me. Then I thought I would have to live forever with an unsaved wife, but God brought you to Himself, and now this. My darling Charlie, I can't tell you how I've dreamed of our going to see my family, and then going to Hawaii to work with Father."

"I know," Charlie whispered softly. "Did you think we could live together as husband and wife without me learning to read your thoughts?"

This caused Sean to laugh deeply, and he wrapped his arms fiercely around her. They prayed together, surrounded by each other's embrace. It was a prayer of surrender for the future, near and far. They both fell quickly asleep, their hearts filled with prayers that God would be glorified in their lives.

The next morning they made their way to the bank. In the space of a few minutes, their hearts at peace, they told Witt they were willing to talk about the sale of the livery.

forty-six

Y̲ou're really leaving, aren't you?"

Charlie nodded and bravely fought the tears that threatened. She knew Sadie had wanted to tell her she couldn't go anywhere, but the fact was, they were leaving in two days and the time for facing reality was at hand.

"What about the baby, Charlie? Should you be traveling when you're so far along?"

"The doctor says I'm in great shape, and we're taking the train for most of the journey."

"You've changed, Charlie." Sadie sounded almost despondent. "I'm not saying it's a bad change; it's just that I don't understand it."

Charlie couldn't bear the dejected look on Sadie's face. Gently grasping her aunt's arm, she led her to the sofa in Sadie's small parlor.

In the minutes that followed, Charlie learned a great deal about her aunt's knowledge of the Bible. She hadn't realized that her late Uncle Harry had read the Bible regularly.

"Your Uncle Harry was a good man, Charlie. He deserved God's love."

"And you don't think you do?" Charlie asked softly.

Sadie let out a small sigh. "I'm nearing 60, honey."

"You're only 56," Charlie replied, wondering why Sadie believed her age mattered.

"Yes, but I've lived those 56 years for myself, and I don't really think God would be interested in me now."

"I don't believe that, Sadie." Charlie spoke with quiet conviction.

"I know you don't. You believe that everyone is redeemable—but I just don't know."

The conversation continued on in this vein for nearly two hours, and even though Sadie listened intently to all Charlie shared, Charlie could see that she was not convinced.

When it came time for Charlie to leave, however, she did not go under a cloud of depression. She believed that God really would save her aunt in His time.

When Sadie saw how much Charlie loved Sean, and how badly she wanted to go and do this "missionary thing," as she called it, Sadie was able to send her with her blessing.

Charlie told her aunt, without offending, that she would be praying for a change in her heart. Knowing that this would be their only private goodbye, their embrace was long and tearful.

❏ ❏ ❏

The church family gave Sean and Charlie a loving send-off. There was a potluck supper, served at the church, the night before they were scheduled to leave. Pastor Miller asked Sean to share his testimony with all present, and Sean praised God for the opportunity to give Him the glory for all that had transpired in the last months.

Most of what he shared regarding his years in Hawaii, his mother and father's departure, and the way his heart turned from God was a surprise to those who attended. The sincerity they saw as he told how God had changed him gained him numerous hugs when he finished and came down into the crowd.

Pastor Miller quieted everyone so he could pray for their journey, and then presented them with a generous gift of money to help them on their way.

The potluck followed and went quite late into the evening. Though it made it hard to rise in the morning, excitement rode them and they rose with hearts of anticipation for the day's travel. Once at the train station, they found Duncan, Lora, and Sadie on hand to see them off. Lora gave them a basket of food for the trip.

Few words were said, but all promised to write, and after a round of hugs was shared and tears were shed, the Donovans were on their way. Charlie didn't cry as Sean had expected. She was very quiet for the first five miles, and Sean didn't press her into conversation. Sometime after the fifth mile, she fell into a sound sleep on Sean's shoulder.

At the end of their first day, they were both sticky with perspiration and felt cramped from sitting so long. But on they rode, taking trains and two stages, whatever was needed to speed them on their journey. Charlie was beginning to think they would never stop moving when the stage they were on pulled into Santa Rosa late one evening. It was after 8:00, so the shipping office and all other businesses were closed for the night. The streets were quiet.

Sean thought Charlie looked about ready to collapse, but she told him it felt so good to stretch her legs that she could ignore the fatigue. They didn't rush their walk, and since they had left their big trunk at the stage office, they had only one small traveling bag each. Once they stood in front of the Riggs' home, Sean paused.

"This is the place."

"It's big, isn't it?"

"I guess it is pretty spacious," Sean agreed, but he didn't speak again or move toward the house.

The last days, as well as the walk from the stage office, were beginning to wear on Charlie, but she sensed Sean needed time, so she stayed quiet. When he finally stepped toward the house, she moved after him, praying that her legs would hold.

Charlie stood behind Sean and watched as a man opened the door, shouted Sean's name, pulled him inside, and grabbed him in a bear hug. Smiling at the sight of the reunion, Charlie was making a move forward when the door was shut, almost in her face.

Strangely enough, Charlie did not feel hurt or rejected. In fact she chuckled just a little. Originally they had planned on Sean coming alone for a visit, returning to Visalia before the baby was born and then heading to Hawaii from there. Charlie knew that none of Sean's family was expecting her.

Charlie mentally counted the seconds before the door was wrenched open. Eight seconds passed before she was once again seeing Sean's face, which registered shock over what had happened.

"I'm sorry," he spoke softly, his expression telling Charlie he was slightly aghast over her being so totally ignored.

"It's all right, Sean," she smiled to reassure him. "But could I please sit down somewhere?"

Sean ushered Charlie into the living room in time to hear Kaitlin scolding Rigg.

"I can't believe you left her standing on the front porch!"

Rigg was fighting laughter. "Honestly, Kate," he tried to placate her, "I didn't see her."

Kate frowned at the sparkle she saw in his eyes before enveloping her new sister-in-law with her embrace.

"Oh, Charlotte, you must be exhausted! Come right over here to the sofa."

Kate then proceeded to issue orders to Rigg and Marcail like a drill sergeant, and within the space of a few seconds Charlie was alone with Sean. Sean smiled at the wide-eyed look on her face.

"She's not always so bossy."

"I think she's wonderful," Charlie whispered as tears filled her eyes. As always, the sight of Charlie's tears melted his heart. He sat beside her and pulled her against him. She didn't cry, but her breathing was uneven and her whole frame shuddered with suppressed sobs.

A few minutes passed, and Sean could tell without looking at her that she was no longer sobbing. That she was asleep was not apparent to him until Marcail came in with a mug of hot coffee. He watched his sister stop halfway across the rug, and then tip-toe to set the cup on the sofa table.

"She's asleep, Sean," Marcail whispered and Sean nodded. "If you want to carry her upstairs, your room is all ready."

"Maybe I'd better."

Kaitlin and Rigg came back in time to see Marc leading Sean up the stairs with his precious bundle. As their feet disappeared from view, Kate spoke.

"I'm so glad they came together, but we didn't even get to meet her."

"We'll have plenty of time for that."

"I almost ran upstairs to wake the girls."

"Since tomorrow is Sunday, we'll all have the entire day to get acquainted."

❑ ❑ ❑

"So tell us your plans!" Rigg encouraged Sean as both men, Katie, and Marcail sat around the kitchen table.

"Well," he said slowly, "I probably should have explained everything to you before moving back, bag and baggage, but—"

"You misunderstand me, Sean," the older man assured him gently. "I'm not trying to pin you down to any schedule. I'm just excited to have you here and want to know what you have in mind."

"I guess I just wanted the baby to be born here," Sean began again. "Everything happened so quickly with the sale of the livery. I know we'd have been welcome at Sadie's if we had to stay, but we honestly believed the trip would be easier for Charlie and the baby *before* the baby was born." Sean's gaze traveled upward to where his wife was sleeping. "She's so tired right now," Sean continued, "I wonder if we made the right decision."

"I think she'll be fine, Sean," Katie told him. "You know that we'll do all we can to make her comfortable. And we're just thrilled that your baby will be born here." Kate's voice caught just a little.

Sean could only nod, his heart full. It had been so long since they'd been together, and so much had passed. Marcail, quiet as she was, seemed to be having the hardest time. She kept touching Sean as though making certain he was really there.

They talked late into the night before Rigg said they'd better get some sleep. No one argued, and after a few yawns and another round of hugs, Sean made his way upstairs.

"Sean?" Charlie's voice was heavy with sleep as she felt the bed shift beside her.

"I'm sorry I woke you."

"What time is it?"

"I'm not sure, I think about 2:00 A.M."

"Oh, Sean," Charlie pleaded as she remembered where she was. "Please tell me I didn't fall asleep before a proper introduction to your family."

Charlie buried her face in the pillow when he laughed softly. Forgetting the hour, she told herself to get up and apologize, but before she could work out the time or force herself out of bed, she was back to sleep.

forty-seven

Charlie looked around the breakfast table at the people surrounding her and smiled. Marshall Riggs, a man whose frame was even larger than Sean's, was a big sweetheart. He had taken Charlie's hand as soon as she had come downstairs and humbly asked her forgiveness for closing her outside in the cold. That he was still amused over what he'd done was immediately evident to her, and they ended up grinning at each other like old friends.

Kaitlin, so obviously Sean's sister, was a model of tenderness. Charlie had apologized about falling asleep, but all Kaitlin did was laugh and hug her again. She then went on to tell Charlie some great stories about the way she had behaved when she was expecting, putting Charlie so at ease that she laughed until she had tears in her eyes.

"Beautiful" was the only word Charlie could mentally formulate to describe Marcail Donovan. Kaitlin was extremely attractive, but Marcail's exquisite features and huge dark eyes were so fetching that Charlie caught herself staring on more than one occasion. Marcail had a genuine desire to help, and her lovely mouth would draw into a smile at the slightest provocation. Her frame and height were petite. Charlie, who never considered herself tall, found that Marcail looked up to her.

The last to come under Charlie's scrutiny were Gretchen and Molly. The sight of them caused Charlie to smile. Both girls were darling, with big dark eyes and the coal-black hair that seemed to be the hallmark of this family. They were perfect little ladies at the breakfast table. Since Gretchen was only four and Molly was just two, Charlie mentally congratulated Rigg and Kate for the work that must have gone into the last years.

There was a bit of a squabble in the wagon on the way to church, showing Charlie that the girls were not always so well behaved. But their quick response when repri-manded, and the way they snuggled close to their Uncle Sean and Aunt Charlotte as if they had known them for years, was enough to win over even the hardest of hearts, let alone one like Charlie's that was waiting to love them.

◻ ◻ ◻

Charlie desperately tried to keep the names of every-one she had met clear in her mind. So many from Rigg's family had come to meet her that she was beginning to think that he was somehow related to the entire church.

"We're all going to Taylors for lunch," Sean told her as the wagon pulled out of the church yard.

"Rigg's family?"

"Right."

"Which ones were they?" Charlie looked very wor-ried.

Sean took her hand and squeezed it. "Don't try to remember. They'll understand if you need to ask their names."

Charlie wasn't at all convinced, and with Molly trying to get Sean's attention, he missed the look of distress on his wife's face.

❑ ❑ ❑

"It's all a little overwhelming, isn't it?"

Charlie turned and found one of Rigg's brothers smiling down at her. He joined her on the sofa, and Charlie gave him a tired smile.

"I've never had any trouble with names before," Charlie stated apologetically.

"I'm Gilbert Taylor, Rigg's brother, and please don't apologize," Gil forestalled her.

Charlie smiled. "I won't, although it seems as though all I've done in the past 24 hours is apologize. Actually," Charlie paused, looking a little surprised, "I haven't been here that many hours." She looked even more exhausted after realizing that less than a day ago she was on a stage just coming into town.

Gilbert, always sensitive to the feelings of others, talked quietly to Charlie until her lids began to droop. The house was noisy, but she fell asleep beside him, and he stayed close to keep the little ones from disturbing her.

It wasn't long before Sean came in from the kitchen. He had been talking with Bill and May Taylor, and Rigg and Kaitlin. When he saw Gilbert guarding Charlie, he grabbed the newspaper and with a softly spoken word of thanks took his place.

Charlie was able to catch almost an hour's sleep before someone slammed a door and woke her. Sean had done very little reading as he sat beside her. He had been praying, and as soon as Charlie's eyes focused on him he spoke to her in a soft tone.

"I think I owe you an apology."

"Over what?" Charlie blinked slowly at him, but she had heard every word.

"About taking you out of the house today, even for church."

"I don't understand what you mean."

"I mean, we're going to be here until after the baby is born, so you'll have lots of time to meet folks. I had no business taking you out today, introducing you to dozens of people, and then bringing you here for lunch, when all you needed was rest."

"I hope you know you're being very silly," Charlie said, her voice still very sleepy. "I wanted to go to church, and you've told me how long all these people have been praying for you. Sean, you *needed* to see them."

Sean only shook his head and moved close enough to put his arm around her. With one arm holding her close, he reached with his free hand to the roundness of her stomach. It seemed she was increasing daily.

While Sean held her close he whispered in her ear that she was the most important person on earth to him. He told her that from now on, he would be taking much better care of her. Charlie tried once again to tell him she was fine, but he silenced her with a kiss.

Neither one of them realized that Kaitlin had come into the room just in time to witness that kiss. She turned back to the kitchen with a smile on her face. The only thing better than having Sean come home was having him home with the woman he loved and who loved him in return.

forty-eight

Charlie had been in Santa Rosa for about eight days when the dam that carefully held her emotions in check shattered. It was a Sunday morning, and while still in the bedroom getting dressed for the day Sean innocently teased her about once again falling asleep when conversation was going on around her.

To Sean's utter amazement, Charlie burst into tears. He apologized several times, but she seemed inconsolable. Staying with her until the harsh sobs had passed, Sean left her still crying softly on the edge of the bed to tell Kate they would not be joining the family for church.

When he returned to the room, he found that she was once again readying for church. In a soft voice Sean told her that he didn't think they should go; they needed some time alone to talk. Sean stood helpless as she once again erupted into tears.

He stood back for only an instant before going to her and taking her in his arms. With gentle movements he removed her dress and slipped her back into the nightgown she had just changed from. Charlie was still crying into the handkerchief that Sean had pressed into her hands when Sean lifted her and put her back beneath the covers of the bed.

He expected her to fall back to sleep immediately, but after some minutes, with her eyes still closed and voice shuddering, she began to speak.

"I can't do it, Sean, I just can't do it. I can't remember anyone's name, and I think they're offended when I forget. My back hurts constantly. And it's almost Christmas! We don't have gifts for anyone. I'm tired all the time. I'm so tired."

Sean listened to all of this in silence and then climbed onto the bed beside her. He smoothed the hair away from her wet cheek and used the handkerchief to dry her face. She had developed a body-shaking case of the hiccups by the time Sean's arms were back around her.

"You're frightened about a lot of things, Charlotte, and I hate to think how long you've been keeping all of this to yourself." His voice was compassionate and coaxing.

"I want you to be proud of me." Her voice faltered with suppressed sobs. "I don't want to do anything to stand in the way of our going to Hawaii."

"No man could be more proud of his wife than I am," he told her with tender assurance. "And as far as Hawaii goes, I'm glad you brought it up because I've been praying about that very subject."

Charlie shifted so she could look at Sean's face. "You've changed your mind? You don't think I'll be a good missionary?"

"You will be a wonderful missionary," he told her with a kiss. "But I don't think there's any hurry. Our money is in the bank, and after Christmas I think we should find a place of our own. That will take the pressure off as to when we should leave. It might be two months after the baby is born, and it might be two years. Rigg has already asked me to work part-time for him at the mercantile, and I don't think I'll have trouble finding other employment."

"But if it weren't for me, you'd leave now?" Charlie looked utterly despondent.

"No, my darling Charlie, I wouldn't. There is still one person whom I haven't even been able to talk with about all of this, and that's my father. His opinion means a lot to me, and I need to write and ask for his counsel. Now, I have a question for you. Are you sorry we left Visalia?"

Charlie answered immediately. "No, in fact I can see why you talk so fondly of Santa Rosa; it's a wonderful town. But I *do* miss Sadie, and my world feels turned on end right now, and—"

She couldn't go on, but she didn't need to; Sean understood completely. They talked until Charlie yawned expansively.

"I'm sorry I'm so tired all the time."

Sean laughed and shook his head. "You're way too hard on yourself. When Katie was pregnant with Gretchen, all she did was sleep. It was even worse with Molly, since she had Gretchen to care for at the same time." Sean kissed her softly. "Go to sleep. When you wake up I'll make you some breakfast."

Charlie was too tired to reply, and almost before Sean could remove his arms from around her she was asleep.

Sean took advantage of the quiet house and sat in the living room to read his Bible. He then spent a long time on his knees praying for Charlie. He asked God to help her to know Him better, and to understand that God's love for her was all-encompassing. He prayed for her physical needs and for those of the baby.

He then went on to pray for himself, especially that he would accept whatever future God had for him. He asked for sensitivity to Charlie's needs, and about when they should move on from Santa Rosa. Still very peaceful about being there, he asked God to show him in an unmistakable way when Hawaii, or anywhere else, was right for them.

Charlie awoke more than an hour later, and after they ate breakfast she and Sean spent some time in prayer before reading the newspaper.

◻︎ ◻︎ ◻︎

The next morning Kaitlin took Charlie to meet Dr. Grade, the doctor who had delivered both Gretchen and Molly. He gave Charlie a good report on the baby's position, as well as a clean bill of health for herself. Kate, who was very cognizant of Charlie's fatigue, watched her face closely when she asked if Charlie wanted to do some Christmas shopping.

"Do you have time?"

"Sure," Kate told her easily. "Sean is playing with the girls, Rigg is working, and Marcail is at school. I have, for the moment, time on my hands." Katie gave a little shrug and Charlie laughed.

The women went to Rigg's Mercantile, and Charlie was able to cover over half of her Christmas list. The only gift she hesitated on was a pair of black stockings for Marcail.

"Won't she be embarrassed to open these in front of everyone?"

Kaitlin chuckled. "Not Marc; she is quite drawn to feminine attire. I promise you, she'll love them."

Kate knew that she still had plenty of time before her girls would even ask about her, but after making her purchases Charlie was flagging. Kate asked if they could finish on another day, and Charlie was more than willing to comply. Their conversation on the walk home was light and carefree.

"I would have said that running a livery was the hardest job on earth," Charlie commented. "But now that I'm pregnant, I've changed my opinion."

"And to think," Kaitlin said with wonder in her voice, "for a while you did both."

"Not really, Katie. Sean has been rather hennish since I fainted on the Fourth of July."

"Well, since you're obviously not a person who will ease up, I can see why."

Charlie knew she was right, so all she did was smile. Kate did not miss that smile. She decided that as soon as she was home, she would have a talk with her brother and sister-in-law.

❑ ❑ ❑

"How did you know we were thinking of moving?" Charlie asked Kaitlin.

"I didn't, not for certain. But Rigg and I talked about it last night. We both think that getting your own place is fine, but we think you should wait until after the baby is born."

Sean and Charlie exchanged a look. He knew Charlie thought she was a great burden because no one let her wash clothes or do work of any kind, but he also remembered how sick his mother had been when they first came to San Francisco. Aunt Maureen had not let her lift a finger. While it couldn't change the fact that she was very ill, it did remove the weight of housework. With the baby coming, it was doubtful that Charlie would have another chance to receive such a rest.

"I think it's a great idea, but I know Charlie is concerned about being a burden."

Charlie gave Sean a look that told him she wished he hadn't said that, but he was not sorry. As he hoped, Kaitlin knew just the right thing to say.

"I can't quite describe to you, Charlie, how long we've waited to see Sean like this. I'm not talking about physically; I'm talking about spiritually. I don't know if you'll understand this, but it's our *privilege* to help you. I think you both need nurturing right now, and the fact that we get to reach out to you means more than I can say."

There was nothing Charlie could say to this, except thanks, and she did. It didn't change her desire to help, and she hoped Katie would agree, but Charlie knew she needed to take herself off and spend some time in prayer.

She put aside her pride and was able to admit to herself how badly she needed the rest they were offering. She also found a verse that became very special to her in the days to come, Philippians 4:19: "But my God shall supply all your need according to his riches in glory by Christ Jesus."

forty-nine

Two days before Christmas Charlie sat in the living room with Gretchen, listening to her chatter on about people whom Charlie thought she remembered *might* be her cousins. Why it was so hard to learn everyone's name and relationship, Charlie was still not sure. To add to the confusion, when Gretchen got excited her speech was not as clear, and names like Cleo, Willy, Joey, Paige, and Sutton flew at her so fast that she couldn't keep them straight.

Marcail entered the room in time to see Charlie looking utterly bewildered. A few minutes later Gretchen jumped down from the couch and went happily on her way. A look of determination crossed Charlie's face. Had Sean seen it, he would have laughed, since it usually meant she had work for him. Marcail smiled in her sweet way, unaware of the fact that Charlie was going to keep her in the living room for the next hour.

"Marcail," Charlie said with quiet determination. "I wonder if you could do me a favor?"

"Sure."

"I'd like you to start at the top and tell me the names of the people in this family. I want to know who Sutton and

Paige are, and all the others. Not just their names, but how they're related to Sean."

Marcail smiled. Charlie looked ready to take the world in her hands. Marcail thought she was wonderful.

"That's a pretty tall order, but I'll give it a try."

Charlie nodded, her brow furrowed in concentration. She made herself a little more comfortable on the sofa, and Marcail began.

"I guess the main family is the Taylors, so I'll start with Bill and May and their kids, the oldest of whom is Rigg. Rigg is a Riggs and not a Taylor because his father died when he was little and May married Bill. You, of course, know who his wife and children are." Marcail waited for Charlie to nod and then moved on.

"Next is Jeff Taylor. His wife is Bobbie, and their children are Cleo and Sutton. Bobbie's parents are Jake and Maryanne Bradford. Bobbie also has an older sister named Alice. Alice and her husband have twins named Paige and Wesley. Bobbie's brother is Troy. Troy is married to Carla, and they have a little boy named Jacob, after his grandpa."

Charlie nodded again, this time with a little more understanding, and Marcail continued.

"After Jeff is Gilbert. You met him two Sundays ago. He's not married and still lives with Bill and May. After Gil comes Nathan. Nathan's wife is Brenda and their little guy is Willy."

"Who is Joey?"

"Oh, Joey Parker," Marcail looked almost apologetic. "He's my age. We go to school together. He's not related to us, but is a good friend of the family. Gretchen talks about him because she thinks he's wonderful."

"Is there anyone who's going to be at Taylors on Christmas Day you haven't mentioned?"

Marcail thought for a moment. "Joey's dad, Mr. Parker, will be there. Not everyone will be there for the meal, Charlotte. Some have other family in town, and they'll just come for dessert."

Charlie smiled at her understanding tone. "Marcail, has anyone told you lately that you're wonderful?"

Marcail only smiled and then looked at the front door as a knock sounded. She made a move to answer it, but Charlie stopped her.

"I'll get it, Marc. I've been sitting too long as it is."

Charlie was a little stiff in her movements as she waddled toward the door, and the person on the other side knocked a second time before she could get there. Charlie swung the door open and even though there was plenty of light, it took her a few moments to respond.

Patrick Donovan's face broke into a huge grin as he took in his daughter-in-law's startled face and swollen form.

"Well now," he spoke softly. "I thought I would be the one doing the surprising, but I can see that the surprise is on me."

Charlie beamed and moved to hug Sean's father. The door opened directly into the living room, so it only took a moment for Marcail to see that her father had arrived. Her happy shout brought the household running.

Patrick was not able to get a word in for some minutes. He was hugged, pulled this way and that, and questioned until he could do nothing but laugh at the pandemonium. When the family settled down, Patrick's gaze settled on his son. Sean smiled at him, but his look turned curious when Patrick continued to stare.

"So tell us how you came to be here," Kaitlin asked when the silence lengthened.

"I think Sean is the only one who can tell me that."

"What do you mean?" Marcail spoke this time.

"Just that I knew I had to come. I knew he planned to be here from Katie's letter and that I had to see him."

This time it was Sean and Charlie who looked at each other. Charlie's face lit with such a peaceful smile that Sean felt his throat close. She knew Sean had written to his father asking how he felt about their coming to Hawaii, but the letter had obviously missed him.

Father and son did not get a chance to talk just then, because both Molly and Gretchen wanted their grandpa's attention, but the adults knew their time would come that evening when the children were in bed.

❑ ❑ ❑

Rigg kissed his wife and thanked her for supper before asking her if she wanted him to play with the girls or do the dishes. Kate was more than ready to give her daughters over to their father, so Rigg ushered them into the living room for games.

They started with "horsey" rides around the room, and when everyone was flushed with laughter, they settled onto the sofa with a book. Patrick and Sean were still in the kitchen with Kate and Marcail. Charlie was in the living room, enjoying the story along with the children.

It seemed like no time at all before the girls were kissing everyone goodnight and being carted off to bed by their loving, but somewhat tuckered, father. Kate served coffee in the living room and when all was quiet, Patrick spoke.

"Knowing how seasick I always become, getting on that boat was the last thing I wanted to do," he admitted softly. "Although I must admit it seemed a little better this time. But no matter; I *had* to come. I didn't even stop to see Maureen. Now, Sean, tell me why I'm here."

"I wrote to you that we were leaving Visalia and coming here, and even though it seems you missed my letter, you would have known that from Kate's." Sean went on to explain how Charlie had come to grips with leaving, Witt's unexpected visit to announce a buyer for the livery, and all the other details leading up to that moment.

"I laid it out in the letter, but the main point was not to give you information, but to ask your advice. Charlie and I value your opinion, and we want to know what you think of our coming to Hawaii to work with you."

Patrick couldn't answer. Sean had shared with him during the summer about this very desire, and Patrick suspected this was the reason it had been so heavy on his heart to be here, but hearing it with his own ears brought him more joy than he thought possible.

"We've prayed for so long that God would send willing workers, Sean." Patrick's voice was thick with emotion. "Come, Sean. Bring your family and come as soon as God leads. I understand that you may want to wait to travel with the baby, but come. We need you in the islands."

Everyone tried to talk at the same time after that. Above the conversation Rigg could be heard telling Sean and Charlie that he wanted them to continue living at the house until they left. When some of the excitement died down, Charlie found herself to be the center of attention.

"Charlotte," Kate implored, "would you mind telling us a little of how you and Sean met?"

Charlie chuckled. "It wasn't exactly what you'd call conventional. In fact, until I came to know the Lord, I couldn't have told you why I was at that hanging, but I see now that it was all a part of His plan."

"When did you fall in love?" Marcail asked with a teenager's curiosity about romance.

"I think it happened for me when Sean punched a man in the face to protect me."

Every mouth in the room dropped open. Charlie and Sean couldn't help grinning at each other, even though it hadn't been at all funny at the time. Everyone in the room was gawking at them. Sean finally took pity on his family and explained. Katie looked ready to punch Murphy herself when she found out he had assaulted Charlie.

The conversation moved to how Sean had spent the years prior to meeting Charlie. His family was at once captivated and grieved for all he had been through because of the choices he made. The last question of the evening came from Patrick, and it was addressed to Charlie.

"How did you come to know that you could move away from your home?"

Charlie smiled at the eldest Donovan. "It was the Lord again. For years I'd been so content, and then I suddenly had this blacksmith to whom I happened to be married, and one of the first things I noticed was how he looked more natural with a Bible in his hand than a hammer. I knew then it was just a matter of time." She paused and turned her smile to Sean. "And now our going to Hawaii—that too I think is just a matter of time."

fifty

The Christmas season passed with a full slate of activities and fun. Sadie's box of gifts was a little late, but it arrived filled with clothes for the baby. Charlie was delighted with each tiny handmade article.

With a prayer in his heart that Sean and family would join him soon, Patrick said goodbye to his family two days after the new year.

When February arrived and her due date was still two weeks away, Charlie became discouraged. She was so big and uncomfortable that it felt as if she would be pregnant forever. She was poised to tell Sean just that when the first contraction hit. Charlie's startled gaze flew to Sean, who was already dressed for church and reading his Bible. He did not immediately notice her distress. She gasped softly as the pain eased, causing Sean to look her way.

"The baby?" Sean's voice was instantly urgent when he saw his wife's horrified face.

"I think so," Charlie said breathlessly.

Sean was out the door and down the stairs to alert his sister before Charlie could make a move. Upon entering the bedroom moments later, Kate hardly had to question

Charlie before telling her to put her nightgown on and get back into bed.

Rigg took the girls and went for his mother. On the way home he stopped to let Dr. Grade know that Charlie's labor had begun. She was in the midst of another contraction when May Taylor walked in. May's countenance was calm, and Charlie found her voice very soothing in the midst of her agony.

Hours passed. Thinking he would burst if he had to watch his wife's suffering for one more moment, Sean was in and out of the room often. He almost wished she would cry out or rail at him, but she bore her pain silently.

The sun was setting when Dr. Grade came for the last time. He told Charlie her delivery would happen any minute, and in less than five, a tiny baby boy slid into his waiting hands.

The room buzzed with activity, and Charlie heard someone calling down the stairs that it was a boy, but beyond that she heard and saw nothing. Her eyes were locked on the tiny, howling infant that was being wrapped in a dry sheet and placed in the crook of her arm.

She ached from head to foot, but at the moment nothing mattered save her baby. She began to croon softly to him and watched in fascination as he stopped crying and turned his face toward hers. The room emptied of everyone but Sean before Charlie looked away from the little boy who had captured her heart with just one glance.

"Isn't he beautiful?" Charlie breathed softly as she held Sean's eyes with her own.

Sean's smile was infinitely tender, but he was actually thinking that their little son was as funny-looking at birth as Gretchen and Molly had been. He sensed immediately that he should keep this particular comment to himself.

"What are we going to call him?" Sean chose a safe subject.

"Ricky," Charlie answered softly.

"Ricky?"

"That's right. It's short for Patrick Sean Donovan IV."

"I like it," Sean said with a smile, thinking he would never have thought of it. In fact, they hadn't even discussed names, and that struck him as being a little unusual.

Sean leaned and kissed his wife to thank her for their son before pressing a kiss to the tiny dark head of his namesake.

"I have a son." Sean said the words aloud as though he was finally believing it. Charlie passed Ricky into his father's arms and watched as tears flooded his eyes. Neither of them spoke for some time after that. It was enough just to sit and watch the tiny movements of the little miracle God had placed within their arms.

□ □ □

In the next several weeks Ricky Donovan grew quickly and seemed to take an unusual interest in his surroundings. He had occasional bouts of colic, but nothing severe. Charlie seemed to have unfailing patience even when he cried for no apparent reason.

Most nights he slept well, and having a good night's sleep was always enough to send Charlie forward for a full day of activity. Sean's family had thought she was wonderful from the day they met, but nothing could have prepared them for a post-pregnant Charlie.

She never sat still. If she wasn't taking care of Ricky, she was mending clothes or baking bread. One day she even went to the livery where Sean had found extra work to lend a helping hand.

After watching Sean and Charlie move nonstop from day to day at what appeared to be their normal activity level, it came as no surprise to the family when Sean announced their plans to leave. Ricky was only four weeks old.

It was the first of March, and Sean said that he would write a letter to Aunt Maureen relaying their plans to be in San Francisco for one week at the end of the month. Everyone understood then that the Sean Donovan family had only three more weeks in Santa Rosa.

As well-prepared as Kaitlin thought she was, she felt bereft at their announcement. It had been so much fun to have them, and she knew it would be at least two years before they would be together again. It therefore came as a surprise to her that she wasn't more upset when the time to say goodbye finally arrived. She strongly suspected that it had plenty to do with the peace and joy she saw glowing from the faces of her brother- and sister-in-law as they boarded the stage. Confidence that they were going exactly where God wanted them to go showed in their every move.

Not only were Sean and Charlie confident, they were thrilled with the idea of going to Hawaii. Sean had been coaching Charlie in the Hawaiian language, and she knew enough to give her a great start once they arrived. A letter had been sent to Father to inform him of their approximate sailing date. The young couple knew there was nothing else they could do except head to San Francisco where they would board a ship that would take them to an exciting new life—a life that Sean knew well, but one that Charlie had only dreamed about. A life of service to their God and prayers that their service would bring honor and glory to His name.

fifty-one

Aunt Maureen, who was not a grandmother herself, fell instantly in love with Ricky. Charlie was rarely able to hold him for the nine days they visited.

Two days before their scheduled departure Sean and Charlie had a "Hawaiian" day. Neither one spoke English, and Sean even attempted to teach Charlie how to cook his favorite Hawaiian dish. They were having a great time, but in one quiet moment Charlie spoke quite seriously, and in English.

"It's all a little like playing house, isn't it? But it won't be all fun and games, will it, Sean? Being missionaries is a lot of hard work."

"That's true, but I think the fact that we're both so burdened to be there means that God will bless and provide for us.

"And Charlie," Sean's voice grew urgent. "This doesn't have to be forever. If we get there and you or Ricky are miserable, then we don't have to stay. Who knows? Maybe I'll be the one who can't take it. It might not be anything like I'm remembering, and if that's the case God will show us where He wants us to be.

"We haven't discussed the way my father left us, at least not in detail. Even though I've forgiven him, I would never follow in his footsteps. We're going to stay together; the three of us are a team. I don't want you to ever forget that."

Charlie was thankful for her husband's words. With a kiss and a whispered word, she let him know of her love for him.

❑ ❑ ❑

Maureen came to the docks to see them off, but the wind was cold and she stayed in her coach as they boarded. Sean had grown very quiet, and Charlie knew that he was remembering how ill he had been on his one previous trip. They talked about a plan of action if Sean was completely out of commission on the ship as he'd been before. Even though Charlie prayed it would be otherwise, she believed she could do what she had to do.

They stayed at the balustrade as the ship pulled away from the dock. Sean held his tiny son, swathed in blankets, close and spoke into his sleeping face.

"We're leaving now, buddy. We're headed to our new home, to Hawaii, where we will serve others and share Christ's love."

Charlie, having heard every word, found her heart swelling with love for this man God had given her. Never did she believe in all her life that she would have the things she had now. Even if God should choose to remove someone or something from her world, she would never again doubt that He was there and that He loved her unconditionally.

Sean looked over to see Charlie's face turned skyward, a look of profound serenity filling her eyes.

"What are you thinking?" he asked softly.

"Only that it's all so wonderful. I never dreamed I would have all that God has given me."

Sean's smile was huge. "And to think that a little over a year ago, we were married strangers."

"Oh, Sean!" Charlie's eyes grew wide as she realized his words were true. Then she grinned and proceeded to tease Sean about one of his favorite sayings. "I guess miracles don't take as long as we once believed."

Epilogue

The half-moon cast a faint glow on Charlie as she waded into the waters of the Pacific Ocean. Sean was already splashing in the light surf, but he stopped to watch her. She had on a light shift that she was again able to use for their private nighttime swims.

It had taken longer after her second pregnancy to fit into that shift, but now that little Callie was three months old, Charlie was slim as a girl once again.

They swam, as was their Sunday night ritual, for the better part of an hour before stopping to talk and play in the waves. Grandpa Patrick was home with the baby and a now two-year-old Ricky, both of whom were asleep, or so their parents hoped.

"What did you think of your father's announcement this morning?"

"I think he did a good job, and I'm certainly glad he warned the two of us about his plans a few days ago."

"But you weren't surprised, were you—not even when he shared with us in private?"

"No, I guess I wasn't."

"I can't imagine being here without your father, but I'm certainly excited about where he's going and the possible impact he could have on Sadie."

"I can't imagine him gone either, but it's time—I can see that. He has been praying about it for the better part of a year. Taking the pulpit for Pastor Miller in Visalia is perfect for his needs right now. It's not a large body of believers, and there are several good leaders."

"To hear you, Sean, you'd think he was an old man."

"No, I know he's not an old man, and he assures me that his health is good, but the work here is so widespread now and he just can't stop himself from putting too much on his plate. Did he show you Marcail's letter?"

"Yes, I read it and I really admire her decision, Sean. She's at the end of her schooling, and her home has been with Rigg and Katie for years. As hard as this will be for her, I have to agree that her place is with your father."

"I think so too. I would guess that she's doing this out of love and respect for Father, since she doesn't know him very well after all these years, but I believe that God will bless her for her actions. Plus, it's always been Marcail's dream to teach school. Father will help her to that end."

"Do you really think he will want her to go to work?"

"I think when he sees how badly she wants to teach, he will. He might be protective of her, but he'll do the right thing."

They continued to discuss Sean's family, Sadie's last letter and need for salvation, the mission work, and a myriad of other subjects during their swim. When it was time to head home, they found their towels on the beach and stood wrapped in the cloths and each other's arms, staring up at the crescent moon.

"I love knowing that no matter what happens, God is in His heaven and loves unfailingly."

"You sound a little worried about the days ahead," Sean whispered.

"Not worried really, just aware that there will be changes in the future."

"The changes will be necessary, including some that will cause pain and take adjustment. But as you said, God is in His heaven, and His sovereign will is always at work. By the way, have I told you lately that you're beautiful?"

Charlie turned her head to stare at Sean, who was still looking at the sky. "Where in the world did that come from?"

He looked down at her then. "I was thinking about it when you stepped into the water and realized I don't tell you often enough."

"Oh, Sean," was all Charlie was able to say before his lips covered her own.

As they walked hand in hand toward their house, Charlie wondered if there was anything more beautiful than being married to the man God has chosen for your life.

Charlie let her mind dwell on the hand that held hers. A hand that swung a hammer with strength and surety, a hand that grasped the Bible with confidence during a sermon, a hand that held their children with tenderness, and a hand that would claim her own with loving care every day of their lives.

Charlie didn't have to speculate for very long as to whether or not there was anything more beautiful. With her hand engulfed within Sean Donovan's, she knew she had her answer.

About the Author

Lori Wick is one of the most versatile Christian fiction writers in the market today. From pioneer fiction to a series set in Victorian England to contemporary writing. Lori's books (over 3.9 million copies in print) are perennial favorites with readers.

Born and raised in Santa Rosa, California, Lori met her husband, Bob, while in Bible college. They and their three children, Timothy, Matthew, and Abigail, make their home in Wisconsin.

HARVEST HOUSE
PUBLISHERS

Current Books by Lori Wick

A Place Called Home Series
A Place Called Home
A Song for Silas
The Long Road Home
A Gathering of Memories

The Californians
Whatever Tomorrow Brings
As Time Goes By
Sean Donovan
Donovan's Daughter

Kensington Chronicles
The Hawk and the Jewel
Wings of the Morning
Who Brings Forth the Wind
The Knight and the Dove

Rocky Mountain Memories
Where the Wild Rose Blooms
Whispers of Moonlight
To Know Her by Name
Promise Me Tomorrow

The Yellow Rose Trilogy
Every Little Thing About You
A Texas Sky
City Girl

English Garden Series
The Proposal
The Rescue
The Visitor
The Pursuit

The Tucker Mills Trilogy
Moonlight on the Millpond
Just Above a Whisper
Leave a Candle Burning

Contemporary Fiction
Sophie's Heart
Pretense
The Princess
Bamboo & Lace
Every Storm
White Chocolate Moments

Harvest House Publishers
For the Best in Inspirational Fiction

Mindy Starns Clark

THE MILLION DOLLAR MYSTERIES SERIES
A Penny for Your Thoughts
Don't Take Any Wooden Nickels
Dime a Dozen
A Quarter for a Kiss
The Buck Stops Here

SMART CHICK MYSTERY SERIES
The Trouble with Tulip
Blind Dates Can Be Murder
Elementary, My Dear Watkins

Roxanne Henke

COMING HOME TO BREWSTER SERIES
After Anne
Finding Ruth
Becoming Olivia
Always Jan
With Love, Libby

Sally John

THE OTHER WAY HOME SERIES
A Journey by Chance
After All These Years
Just to See You Smile
The Winding Road Home

IN A HEARTBEAT SERIES
In a Heartbeat
Flash Point
Moment of Truth

THE BEACH HOUSE SERIES
The Beach House
Castles in the Sand

Susan Meissner
Why the Sky Is Blue
A Window to the World
Remedy for Regret
In All Deep Places
A Seahorse in the Thames

Craig Parshall
Trial by Ordeal

CHAMBERS OF JUSTICE SERIES
The Resurrection File
Custody of the State
The Accused
Missing Witness
The Last Judgement

Debra White Smith

THE AUSTEN SERIES
First Impressions
Reason and Romance
Central Park
Northpointe Chalet
Amanda
Possibilities

Lori Wick

THE TUCKER MILLS TRILOGY
Moonlight on the Millpond
Just Above a Whisper
Leave a Candle Burning

THE ENGLISH GARDEN SERIES
The Proposal
The Rescue
The Visitor
The Pursuit

THE YELLOW ROSE TRILOGY
Every Little Thing About You
A Texas Sky
City Girl

CONTEMPORARY FICTION
Bamboo & Lace
Every Storm
Pretense
The Princess
Sophie's Heart
White Chocolate Moments